Mermaid Tales
3-Books-in-1!

★ Also by ★
Debbie Dadey

MERMAID TALES

Coming Soon

Mermaid Tales

Debbie Dadey

Illustrated by
Tatevik Avakyan

3-Books-in-1!

Trouble at Trident Academy * Battle of the Best Friends *
A Whale of a Tale

ALADDIN

NEW YORK   LONDON   TORONTO   SYDNEY   NEW DELHI

ALADDIN

An imprint of Simon & Schuster Children's Publishing Division
1230 Avenue of the Americas, New York, NY 10020
This Aladdin paperback edition August 2016
Trouble at Trident Academy text copyright © 2012 by Debbie Dadey
Trouble at Trident Academy illustrations copyright © 2012 by Tatevik Avakyan
Battle of the Best Friends text copyright © 2012 by Debbie Dadey
Battle of the Best Friends illustrations copyright © 2012 by Tatevik Avakyan
A Whale of a Tale text copyright © 2012 by Debbie Dadey
A Whale of a Tale illustrations copyright © 2012 by Tatevik Avakyan
All rights reserved, including the right of reproduction in whole or in part in any form.
ALADDIN is a trademark of Simon & Schuster, Inc., and related logo
is a registered trademark of Simon & Schuster, Inc.
For information about special discounts for bulk purchases, please contact Simon & Schuster
Special Sales at 1-866-506-1949 or business@simonandschuster.com.
The Simon & Schuster Speakers Bureau can bring authors to your live event.
For more information or to book an event contact the Simon & Schuster Speakers Bureau
at 1-866-248-3049 or visit our website at www.simonspeakers.com.
Series designed by Karin Paprocki
The text of this book was set in Belucian Book.
Manufactured in the United States of America 0716 OFF
2 4 6 8 10 9 7 5 3 1
This book has been cataloged with the Library of Congress.
ISBN 978-1-4814-8555-5
ISBN 978-1-4424-2981-9 (*Trouble at Trident Academy* eBook)
ISBN 978-1-4424-2983-3 (*Battle of the Best Friends* eBook)
ISBN 978-1-4424-2985-7 (*A Whale of a Tale* eBook)
These titles were previously published individually in hardcover and paperback by Aladdin.

Contents

Trouble at Trident Academy

To my wonderful family:
Eric, Nathan, Becky, and Alex.
I look forward to many
more ocean trips together!

★ ★ ★ ★

Acknowledgments

Thanks to Fiona Simpson, Karen Nagel,

and Bethany Buck for letting me swim

with the mermaids!

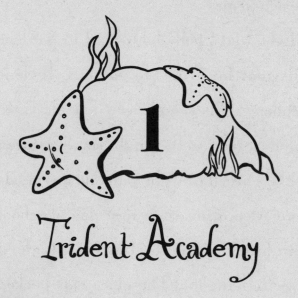

Trident Academy

I CAN'T BELIEVE IT!" ECHO SAID. "IT'S finally happening."

Shelly took a small sip of her seaweed juice before pushing a lock of red hair from her face. Usually she didn't care if her hair stuck straight up, but today was special. "We're so lucky to get an invitation to Trident Academy. I didn't think it would happen to me."

Echo and Shelly both lived in Trident City, not far from the famous Trident Academy. They had been friends since they'd played together in the small-fry area of MerPark. The eight-year-old mermaids were celebrating their first day of school with breakfast at the Big Rock Café, a favorite hangout. The place was packed with students proudly wearing their Trident Academy sashes. The two mergirls didn't see a third mergirl swimming up behind them. Her name was Pearl. Echo and Shelly usually tried to avoid the bossy mergirl from their neighborhood.

"Oh my Neptune!" Pearl snapped when

she saw Shelly. "I can't believe *you*, of all merpeople, got into Trident." Usually only very wealthy or extremely smart students were accepted. Pearl was rich. Echo was a quick learner. Shelly was neither, but she knew more about ocean animals than both of them put together.

Echo came to her friend's defense. "Of course Shelly got into Trident. She is very talented."

"At *what*?" Pearl asked. "Digging for crabs?"

Shelly glanced at her dirty fingernails and immediately hid them under her blue tail fin. "At least I know *how* to hunt crabs. I bet you'd starve to death if you had to do something for yourself."

Pearl flipped her blond hair, stuck her pointy nose up in the water, and said, "I know how to do plenty of things."

"Name one," Shelly said.

"How to be on time for school, for starters," she said. Pearl spun around and flicked her gold tail, knocking seaweed juice all over Shelly's new Trident sash!

Splash!

Pearl giggled and swam off toward school.

"Oh no!" Shelly squealed, dabbing green juice off the gold-and-blue sash. "She did that on purpose!"

Echo glared after Pearl before helping her friend wipe the sash. "It's fine now. You can hardly see it," Echo said. That wasn't *exactly* true—there was definitely a green blob on Shelly's sash.

"We'd better get going," Echo said, adjusting the glittering plankton bow in her dark curly hair. "We don't want to be late on our first day."

Shelly groaned. She wasn't quite so excited now. "If Trident Academy is filled with merpeople like Pearl, then I don't think I'm going to like it."

"There's only one way to find out," Echo said, taking a deep breath. "Let's go."

Burps

"Wow," SHELLY SAID, staring up at the ceiling of the huge clamshell. "This is amazing." Only a few shells in the ocean had ever grown as large as Trident Academy. The front hall alone could fit a humpback whale, and the ceiling was filled with colorful old carvings that showed the history of the merpeople.

"It's awesome, but we'd better get to class," Echo said, grabbing Shelly's elbow. "Third graders are down this way." Echo's older sister went to Trident Academy, so Echo already knew a lot about the school.

Shelly didn't think she'd ever seen so many merpeople in one place. Hundreds of students swam quickly through the massive shell, looking for their classrooms. Each wore a different-colored sash for their grade, from third to tenth.

"Here's our room," Echo said. She shoved aside a seaweed curtain and disappeared inside.

Shelly gulped and followed her friend.

She hoped Pearl wouldn't be in their classroom, but as she entered the class . . .

"Oh no. Did a stinkfish just swim in?" Pearl snapped as she sat at a rock desk.

"No," said a merboy with a big head. "But a burpfish did." He let out a big, long burp right in Pearl's face.

"That is so disgusting, Rocky," Pearl said. "Didn't your parents teach you any manners?"

"I'll tell you what's really disgusting," Rocky said. "That jewelry you're wearing."

Pearl shook her head. "My pearls are *sooooo* beautiful." She ran her fingers over the long necklace.

"Actually," a tiny, dark-haired mergirl said, "pearls *are* sort of disgusting. They're made when an oyster or mussel secretes nacre around an irritant."

Pearl sniffed at the tiny mergirl. "So what?"

"Secretes?" another merboy asked. "What's that?"

"Kind of like spitting," the mergirl explained.

"I knew that," Rocky said with a grin. "That means she's wearing puke around her neck." Several merboys and mergirls in the class giggled at the joke.

The small mergirl nodded, and Shelly took a closer look at her. She had long black hair that reached all the way to her tail; wide, dark eyes; and the palest of skin. Her mertail was a brilliant purple, unlike any Shelly'd ever seen. Shelly's own tail was blue, and Echo's was pink. The mergirl with the purple tail didn't look even a little bit afraid of Pearl. Anyone who could stand up to Pearl was awesome. Shelly knew she was going to like this mergirl.

"Watch this!" Rocky said. He spit into the water around Pearl. At that moment a tall, thin teacher with green hair and a white tail swam into the room. "Young merboy," she asked, "*what* are you doing?"

Rocky grinned. "I'm . . . I'm . . . I'm seeing if I can turn her into a giant glob of spit."

Shelly hid a giggle. She was pretty sure she liked Rocky, too. Maybe Trident Academy wouldn't be so bad after all.

3

Mrs. Karp

GOOD MORNING, STUDENTS. Welcome to Trident Academy. My name is Mrs. Karp," said their teacher. "I will be teaching you reading, storytelling, and science. I trust your parents have started your education and we'll be able to move along quickly."

Shelly squirmed in her sponge seat. Her parents had died when she was just a small fry, and she lived with her grandfather in an apartment above the People Museum. She hoped he'd taught her all she needed to know, since Trident Academy expected their students to have been home-schooled for two years.

All merkids were taught at home until third grade. Sometimes her grandfather was a little forgetful, and some days he hadn't remembered about Shelly's lessons. And Shelly hadn't reminded him. She'd much rather explore underwater caves or play with sea turtles than sit still for lessons.

"Mr. Bottom will teach you math,

life-saving, and astronomy," Mrs. Karp continued.

Rocky snickered at the name Mr. Bottom, but Mrs. Karp silenced him with a glare. "Trident Academy is lucky to have other special teachers that you'll meet later this week. Today we will get to know each other better and start your first project."

Pearl gasped and raised her hand. "What do we have to do?"

Mrs. Karp smiled at the classroom of twenty mergirls and merboys. "I'm glad you are eager to get right to your studies. Your first assignment at Trident Academy will be a report on krill and shrimp."

Shelly groaned quietly. There were so

many exciting things to learn about, like the dolphins and whales she wanted to swim with. Why did they have to learn about silly little shrimp?

"As you know, many sea creatures, including us, would not live long without krill to eat. Why, even humans are known to eat krill, especially those who live near Kiki's far-off waters." Mrs. Karp nodded toward the mergirl who had stood up to Pearl.

Far-off waters? Shelly thought. She was even more curious about Kiki now.

"You will need to collect at least four types of krill or shrimp and complete a seaweed and octopus-ink study on each of them." Merkids used orange sea pens with their sharpened ends dipped in octopus ink to write on neatly cut pieces of seaweed for their studies.

"How many pieces of seaweed?" asked a large mergirl in the back of the room.

"At least one per krill or shrimp," answered Mrs. Karp.

Groans came from throughout the class. "The wise merstudent will start right away," Mrs. Karp told them. "In fact, we will go to the library until lunchtime so you may begin your reports."

Echo leaned over to Shelly. "Want to work together?" she asked.

Shelly nodded. This was their first

project for Trident Academy. She didn't want to mess it up.

As they floated down the hall toward the school library, Echo pointed to the Trident Academy message board. There were notices posted all over it, inviting students to join different clubs.

Shelly noticed a sign written in big green letters:

SHELL WARS PRACTICE
AFTER SCHOOL TODAY
IN MERPARK

Shelly smiled. Shell Wars! She loved playing Shell Wars. Maybe she could make the school team! The rush of water around her face when she scored a goal was a lot more exciting than learning about krill. In her mind, she was already smacking a shell around.

"I want to be one of those," Echo said, pointing to a message about the Tail Flippers, a group that cheered for sporting events.

Shelly nodded. "That looks great. But I think I'll try out for Shell Wars."

"Me too," Kiki said from behind them, and Shelly gave her a big smile.

Pearl swam up beside the mergirls. "Shell Wars is disgusting. I'd never try out for anything so rough."

Shelly and Echo ignored Pearl as they passed a dark gray merman with a huge frown on his face. He looked so sad, Shelly felt like crying. "Who is that?" she whispered.

"I bet that's Mr. Fangtooth," Echo whispered back. "My sister told me all about him. He works in the cafeteria."

"I heard he's a grouch," Pearl said, "and he hasn't smiled in forty years."

"Maybe he just needs cheering up," Shelly said, immediately feeling sorry for Mr. Fangtooth. "I bet Echo and I could make him smile."

"Okay," Pearl said. "It's a bet."

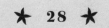

The Bet

IF YOU WERE GRUMPY, WHAT WOULD cheer you up?" Shelly asked Echo as they ate their lunch later that day.

Echo thought about it for a few minutes. "If I found something human," she admitted.

Shelly sighed. She didn't understand her friend's fascination with anything that had to do with humans. Shelly thought killer whales were much more interesting.

Echo swallowed a handful of tiny octopus legs before licking her fingers. "Maybe we could try making funny faces at Mr. Fangtooth. That always makes my dad smile."

Shelly grinned. "What a great idea. Let's put our lunch trays away and make faces at him."

Echo and Shelly stood at the service window of the cafeteria kitchen. Shelly crossed her blue eyes and pushed her nose up against it to look like a dog fish. Echo pulled her dark hair into tall points and puffed her cheeks out. Mr. Fangtooth frowned at them.

Echo blew out the air in her cheeks, making lots of little bubbles. "Why didn't he smile?" she whispered. "That always works with my dad."

"I have the feeling that Mr. Fangtooth hasn't smiled in a very, very long time. I think we're going to have to do something drastic," Shelly said.

"Like what?" Echo asked.

Shelly shrugged and looked around the cafeteria at the scenes of merfolk history carved on the walls. Merstudents of all ages talked and ate their school lunches at polished granite tables with the gold Trident Academy logo in their centers.

Shelly saw Kiki sitting with Pearl and a group of mergirls. Kiki smiled at Shelly, and Shelly gave a little wave, wishing she had thought to invite Kiki to sit with them. Then she turned back to Mr. Fangtooth.

Mr. Fangtooth made a horrible face and bellowed at the mergirls. *Roar!*

Echo screamed and fell right into Rocky. His plate of ribbon worms flew onto Echo's hair.

"*Eeewww!* Get them off!" Echo squealed. Shelly quickly began pulling the long, thin, black-and-white worms out of Echo's curly hair. She stopped when she heard a booming sound.

It was Mr. Fangtooth! His laughter rocked the cafeteria.

All the students looked up from their lunches to see what was happening. Pearl glared at Shelly. "See?" Shelly said. "I told you we could make Mr. Fangtooth laugh. We win the bet!"

Pearl opened her mouth, but she didn't get the chance to talk because Headmaster Hermit's voice came over the conch shell: "Shelly Siren and Echo Reef, please report to the headmaster's office immediately."

"Ooooh," Rocky teased. "You're in big trouble now."

Shelly gulped. It was only her first day at Trident Academy. Now she was worried it would also be her last.

Disaster

"IT WAS HORRIBLE," ECHO TOLD HER older sister, Crystal, later that afternoon at their shell. "I thought for sure we were going to get kicked out of Trident Academy on our first day!"

Crystal shook her head. "You shouldn't have made faces at Mr. Fangtooth. Then you wouldn't have ended up with worms in your hair. The headmaster has spies everywhere, so you have to behave yourselves."

"We were only trying to cheer up Mr. Fangtooth," Shelly explained.

"You'd better stay out of trouble," Crystal warned.

"That's why I'm here," Shelly said. "We're going to work on our project so we'll get finished early."

"That's great," Crystal said. "I can help you if you'd like."

"That's really nice of—" Shelly started to say.

"But we have something else to do first," Echo interrupted her friend.

Crystal shrugged. "Okay. I have to work at the store soon anyway. Good luck." Crystal and Echo's dad ran Reef's Fish Store, which sold small exotic sea creatures of all kinds. Crystal quickly left, and Shelly worried that her feelings were hurt.

"Maybe we should have let her help," Shelly said.

Echo shook her head. "No, Crystal just wants to boss me around. It's a pain having an older sister."

Shelly was an only child, so she thought it would be great to have a brother or sister.

"Besides," Echo said, "I want to show you what I can do." She did a huge backward flip and twisted to the left and right.

"Watch out!" Shelly yelled, and fell sideways, knocking a beautiful glass vase off a turtle shell table. The vase broke into a million pieces.

Echo's tail did even more damage. She whacked three glowing jellyfish lamps, which rolled across the room. The jellyfish shrugged at Echo and swam out of the shell. Once they left, Echo's living room got much darker. The only light came from a row of shining plankton that lined the bottom of the shell.

"Oh, I'm so sorry," Shelly said. "I didn't mean to break your vase. Echo, I can't do anything right. I should just quit everything, including Trident Academy. I know I won't be able to do all the projects, and I sure won't be able to make the Shell Wars team."

Echo swam through the darkened room to grab her friend by the arm. "Don't be silly. I was the one who caused this disaster. It was all because I wanted to practice for Tail Flippers."

"You did a great flip," Shelly admitted. "You just needed more room." Shelly was right. Echo's shell was full of people-junk that she'd collected.

But Echo shook her head. "There's another problem," she said.

"What's that?" Shelly asked. "I'm sure you'll make the team."

Echo slowly lifted her pink tail so her friend could see. A huge black pot was stuck on the bottom. "Help me get it off, Shelly. I can't go to Trident Academy with this on my tail!"

Shelly tried hard not to laugh as she helped her friend. She pulled. She tugged. She smacked the pot with her own tail. Shelly poured kelp oil into the pot and tugged even harder. Nothing worked. The pot was stuck fast on Echo's tail.

Echo started crying. "What am I going to do?"

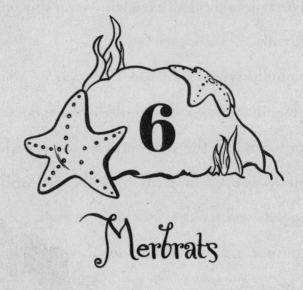

Merbrats

THE NEXT MORNING, SHELLY sped through the water. She hurried past an older merwoman, who raised her fist in disgust. "Young merbrats think they can just knock over anyone in their way."

"So sorry!" Shelly apologized to the

woman, who had only been splashed a bit.
"I can't be late."

"Rush, rush, rush," the old merwoman complained. "Why is everyone in such a big hurry, anyway?"

It was almost time for their second day of school. Shelly had to find out if Echo's parents had been able to remove the pot from her tail. Echo had been so upset yesterday, they hadn't even worked on their krill project, and Shelly was worried they were going to be behind the rest of the class.

She was meeting Echo outside her shell so they could swim to school together. Hopefully the pot was gone and nothing else would go wrong! But when Shelly arrived, Echo's red eyes told her everything.

"They couldn't get it off! This is the worst thing that could have happened to me."

Shelly hugged her friend. She didn't think a pot on her tail was the *worst* that could happen, but it *was* pretty bad. "Maybe you could put something over it?" she suggested.

Echo thought for a moment, then smiled. "That's a great idea. Maybe this will work." She reached into a pile near her front door and pulled out a piece of glittery material.

"What's that?" Shelly asked.

"I found it last week. My dad said he thought it was called 'cloth.' People wear it," Echo explained as she wrapped the sparkly material around her tail *and* the black pot.

Shelly rolled her eyes. More people stuff! She thought shells and woven seaweed made perfectly fine clothing, but she had to admit, the sparkly cloth looked pretty. "You look fabulous!" she told Echo.

"Really?"

"Pearl will probably be jealous," Shelly said. "Now let's hurry or we'll be late." It was hard for Echo to swim fast with her tail all wrapped up, so Shelly pulled her along. They made it to school just as the conch horn sounded.

In class, Mrs. Karp held up a small, almost-see-through creature. "Who can tell me what this is?"

Rocky's hand shot up immediately, and Mrs. Karp nodded toward him. "Lunch!" he exclaimed.

Mrs. Karp frowned and nodded at Pearl. "That is an Antarctic krill," Pearl said smugly. "It is the main food of the blue whale."

Mrs. Karp pointed at Kiki. "Can you add anything to Pearl's explanation?"

Kiki stood on her tail and spouted off information. "Krill are shrimplike crustaceans that form a large part of the zooplankton and our food chain."

"What did she say?" Rocky asked. "What's a zooplankton?"

Shelly wondered the same thing, but Mrs. Karp continued with the lesson.

"Very good," Mrs. Karp told Kiki. "Now, who can pick out other crustaceans from this aquarium?" Mrs. Karp tapped a glass box that was filled with different sea creatures. Shelly knew about most large sea life, but she wasn't sure what a crustacean was, so she looked down at her tail. When no one raised their hand, Mrs. Karp called on Echo.

Oh no, thought Shelly. She was afraid the other merkids would tease Echo if they saw the pot. She held her breath as Echo floated to the front of the room. "Look at her tail," several students whispered as Echo swam by.

But then Kiki said, "It's so pretty."

Another girl named Morgan added, "And so shiny."

Shelly relaxed. Everyone liked Echo's cloth. Everything was going to be fine. But then Echo's tail banged on the teacher's marble desk. *Boing!* The pot made a horrible noise.

"Echo has a musical tail!" a boy named Adam yelled. The class laughed, and Echo's face turned bright red. For a terrible moment Shelly thought that Echo would rush away, but thankfully Mrs. Karp silenced the class.

The rest of the morning was pretty

uneventful until lunchtime. All the mer-girls in the class swarmed around Echo. "Where did you get that? What's it called?" one asked.

Echo smiled and patiently answered all their questions, but she ate lunch with just Shelly. "Whew, I'm glad they didn't see the pot," Echo whispered.

In fact, Echo made it through the rest of the day without any problems.

AFTER SCHOOL ON THE WAY TO MERPARK, Shelly told Echo, "If you don't mind waiting, I'll help you swim home after Shell Wars practice."

"Thanks," Echo said. "If I can't try out for Tail Flippers, at least I can cheer you on."

Shelly felt bad. It didn't seem fair for her to try out for Shell Wars if Echo couldn't be a Tail Flipper. Maybe she should sit with Echo instead of practicing. Shelly started to tell her friend that she'd changed her mind about trying out, but then she had an idea. If her plan worked, it would solve everything.

Harlequin Shrimp

DID YOU SEE THAT?" SHELLY asked Echo. The two mer-girls were swimming over to Shelly's home after Shell Wars practice. Actually, Shelly swam slowly and pulled Echo along.

"I think that's a harlequin shrimp," Echo said, pointing to a blue-and-white-spotted creature. "It's just like the picture in the dictionary. Quick, catch it for our report!"

Shelly did hurry, but she wasn't fast enough. Rocky came out of nowhere and snatched up the shrimp, along with the starfish it was eating.

"Hey, that was ours!" Shelly complained.

Rocky laughed and swam off with the bright blue-and-white shrimp. "Not anymore."

Shelly wanted to chase him, but she swam back to where Echo waited.

"Did you get it?" Echo asked.

"No," Shelly answered. "Rocky did."

"I used to think he was cute, but not now," Echo said.

Shelly giggled. "Who? The harlequin shrimp or Rocky?" she teased.

Echo laughed. "Rocky, silly."

"You thought Rocky was cute?" Shelly asked.

"A little bit," Echo said with a shrug.

"Let's go," Shelly said. "But keep your eyes open for sea cucumbers. Mrs. Karp told me that emperor shrimp live on them. The more shrimp we collect, the better grade we'll get."

The friends looked for specimens. They saw a hammerhead shark's shadow and huge vent tube worms, but no shrimp or krill.

"Look over there," Echo said.

"Is it an emperor shrimp?" Shelly asked.

"No, it's Mr. Fangtooth," Echo whispered. The mergirls hid behind a merstatue as Mr. Fangtooth wiggled toward the Big Rock Café. Through the open windows they watched as he sat at a table by himself, and a merwaitress brought him food.

"He looks so sad," Echo said, peeking around the merstatue.

"Maybe he doesn't have a family to cheer him up," Shelly said. She was grateful she had her grandfather.

"At least we got him to smile yesterday," Echo said.

"And we were sent to the headmaster's office for it," Shelly reminded her.

Echo nodded. "Still, maybe we could make him smile again, and keep him smiling."

"That'd be nice, as long as we don't get in trouble," Shelly said. "I like Mr. Fangtooth a whole lot better than I like Pearl."

"Pearl was bragging about how great

her report was going to be," Echo said. "I don't think it's nice to brag."

"It isn't," Shelly said. "But we'd better get to work on our reports. Let's go to my house." Shelly didn't tell Echo about her plan, but she secretly hoped her grandfather could get the pot off Echo's tail.

"Maybe your grandfather can help us with our reports," Echo said.

Shelly shook her head. "No, we have to do it on our own." If Echo wouldn't let her sister help, why should they ask Shelly's grandfather?

"I bet your grandfather would like to help with our schoolwork," Echo said.

"Sure he would," Shelly said. "But we should do this without him."

"Why?" Echo asked. "He's really smart. And we could get a good grade."

Shelly rolled her eyes. Her whole life, people had been telling her how amazing her grandfather was. She loved her grandfather, but she liked doing things on her own. "No, I don't want to ask him."

Echo put her right hand on her right hip and banged the pot on the seafloor. "Well, I want to."

Shelly scrunched up her nose. Usually she agreed with Echo, but just then she was tired and grouchy. "Well, I don't."

"I do!" Echo yelled.

"I don't!" Shelly yelled back.

"Then I don't want to work with you!" Echo shouted.

"Then I don't want to work with you, either!" Shelly shouted back.

Echo swam away as fast as she could with the pot on her tail. *Bump. Bump. Bump.* The pot thumped along the ocean floor.

Shelly wanted to swim after her friend and tell her she was sorry. But she didn't. "I never even got to tell her my plan," Shelly said to herself. She had the horrible feeling that she'd never be friends with Echo again.

Pearl

I DON'T BELIEVE IT!" SHELLY GASPED. It was the next morning. She had decided to stop by Echo's shell to apologize and help her friend get to school. But Echo wasn't alone. *Pearl* was holding Echo's hand and helping her. Tied around Pearl's tail was a smaller, but still sparkling, piece of cloth just like Echo's. Shelly wondered where Pearl had managed to get the fabric.

Shelly waited behind a kelp plant in MerPark to let Echo and Pearl pass. "I have only one page finished for my report," Echo admitted.

"I haven't started yet," Pearl said.

"You haven't?" Echo asked.

"No, but I'm not worried," Pearl said. "My dad promised to get me some shrimp. And if I were you, I'd just get your father to bring some home from his store. Reef's has tons of shrimp and krill."

"I never thought about that," Echo said.

"You'd be silly not to ask him for help," Pearl said. "It'd be so easy."

Echo nodded. "Maybe. My dad does have lots of neat shrimp, but I don't know if he would give me any."

"You could take them when he wasn't looking," Pearl said.

"That would be stealing!" Echo said.

"No, it wouldn't. It's your store too, isn't it?" Pearl asked.

Echo frowned. "I guess you are right."

"Of course I'm right," Pearl said. "Now let's get to Trident Academy."

Shelly watched her best friend swim away with Pearl. When they were out of sight, Shelly floated slowly to school. All she could think about was Pearl teaching Echo how to do terrible things. Somehow Shelly had to find a way to get Echo away from Pearl.

But Pearl sat next to Echo in the library. Pearl sat next to Echo in the lunchroom. Shelly looked to see if Echo wanted to make Mr. Fangtooth laugh, but Echo didn't even glance Shelly's way. Shelly swam over to an empty granite table in the corner and sat by herself.

"Hi," said a small voice. Shelly looked up from her lunch of leftover clam casserole to find Kiki. "May I sit here?" Kiki asked.

"Sure," Shelly said. "How do you like Trident Academy?"

Kiki shrugged and sat down. "It's okay, but I miss my parents and brothers."

"How many brothers do you have?" Shelly asked.

"Seventeen," Kiki said.

"*Seventeen!*" Shelly shrieked. "Are you kidding me?"

Kiki laughed. "No, I really do have seventeen brothers and not one sister."

"I don't have any brothers or sisters, but I'd like some," Shelly told her.

"It's okay, but very noisy. I always thought I wanted to go somewhere quieter, but the dorm rooms at Trident Academy are almost too quiet in the afternoon."

"Wow, you live in the school dorm?" Shelly asked. "That sounds so cool."

Kiki shook her head and whispered, "I have Wanda for a roommate. She snores really loudly."

Shelly laughed, and out of the corner of her eye she saw Echo look at her. Echo frowned and said something to Pearl and the other mergirls at her table. They all looked in Shelly's direction and burst out laughing. Shelly had a terrible feeling they were laughing at her.

AFTER SCHOOL, SHELLY FLOATED OVER to Shell Wars practice. Kiki was already warming up by gently tossing a shell back and forth with a group of merkids. Kiki waved as Shelly took her place on the field.

In Shell Wars, two teams try to shoot a small shell into the other team's treasure chest and whoever scores more goals wins. Each chest is guarded by a goalie, which just happens to be an octopus! The players use long whale bones to slam the shells with all their might! If anyone touches a shell with their hands or body, they're out of the game, so it's important to pay attention.

"Watch out!" Kiki yelled.

Whack! The shell hit Shelly right in the stomach. She hit the ocean floor hard.

"Oh my gosh!" Echo screamed. "Is she hurt?"

"Serves her right," Pearl snapped. "Shell Wars is a gross game. Who wants to play with a dirty old shell?"

"I might not like Shell Wars, but Shelly does, and she's my friend," Echo said, swimming away from Pearl.

"Are you all right?" Echo asked Shelly as she sat up.

Shelly held her stomach, but she smiled. "I am if we're friends again."

"Are we friends again?" Echo asked.

Shelly nodded, and the two mergirls

★ 67 ★

hugged. Pearl stuck her nose up in the water and swam home alone.

"You want to come over to my house after practice?" Shelly asked Echo.

Echo nodded and giggled. "I'm so glad we're not mad at each other anymore." The friends hugged again before Shelly went back to practice and Echo sat down to watch.

Neither mergirl noticed that Kiki had come over to check on Shelly as well. They didn't see Kiki standing beside them. Neither one noticed when she swam away either. "It's like they ignored me on purpose. I didn't mean to hit Shelly," Kiki whispered. She floated off with tears in her eyes.

9

A Neat Trick

ECHO WATCHED THE REST OF Shell Wars practice. She had to admit that Shelly was good—probably even better than Rocky, and he boasted that he was the best player in the whole ocean.

"You're awesome," Echo told her friend as the merkids finished scrimmaging and Shelly swam over to the sidelines.

"Thanks. I really hope I can make the team! Now let's go to my shell to work on our projects," Shelly suggested, giving Echo's arm a little tug. As the girls swam by a cluster of sea lilies, they didn't realize that Echo's sparkly cloth was caught. In one quick merminute, it fell off and the teasing began.

"Echo has a pot tail!" yelled Rocky. Several other merboys and mergirls followed Rocky's pointing finger to the black pot still stuck on Echo's tail.

"Pot Tail! Pot Tail!" Rocky called after her.

Shelly wanted to bang the pot on Rocky's

head, but she needed to get Echo away from his teasing, so she swam quickly toward home, pulling Echo with her.

"I'm so embarrassed," Echo said when they were safely inside Shelly's apartment.

"Don't worry about it," Shelly said. "If Pearl had seen it, she'd be wearing a pot on her tail tomorrow too."

Echo wiped away a tear. "Do you really think so?"

Shelly nodded. "She wore a sparkly cloth today, didn't she?"

Echo laughed. "That's right, she did."

"I bet my grandfather can get that pot off," Shelly said, finally glad to be telling Echo her plan.

"That's a great idea!" Echo yelled. "He

is, after all, an expert on human things."

Shelly shrugged. Not only was Echo fascinated with human stuff, but so was Shelly's grandfather. He was the director of the People Museum and knew more than anyone in Trident City about human beings and what went on above the sea. There had been many afternoons when Echo had been content to wander around the museum with Shelly's grandpa, looking at useless human tools. But Shelly had been bored to tears.

"And if he can't get your pot off, then I'll find one to put on my tail so we'll match," Shelly said. "We'll have a pot-tail club."

Echo smiled at her friend. "You are the best merfriend in the whole world."

"Come on, let's go find Grandpa," Shelly said.

GRANDPA SIREN TOOK ONE LOOK AT ECHO'S tail and grinned. "Are you sure you want it off? You never know when a good pot could come in handy."

"Grandpa! She really wants it off," Shelly pleaded.

Grandpa Siren rubbed his chin. "I wonder...," he said as he floated off to his storeroom of extra human gadgets.

Bang! Crash! Bang!

"What's he doing in there?" Echo asked.

Shelly shrugged. Her grandpa came out of the storage area with a large wire basket full of small glass bottles, which

he immediately began searching through.

Echo picked one up labeled DANGER: MOTOR OIL. "Will this help me?" she asked.

Grandpa immediately snatched the bottle away. "It would help, but it would also pollute our water. It's deadly to ocean life."

Echo gulped and backed away from the bottles. Grandpa continued looking until he held one up. "This should do the trick."

He poured the tiniest amount of yellow liquid over Echo's tail, and immediately the water filled with round blobs that bounced off each other. "What *is* this stuff?" Echo asked.

"Vegetable oil," Grandpa explained. "I just applied a drop, but I think it worked."

Echo squealed as the pot slid off her tail.

She gave Grandfather a hug. "You're the greatest!"

"Now we can finish our projects," Shelly said. "And look! You've *already* caught two shrimp." Sure enough, two glowing hinge-beak shrimp floated in the bottom of the pot.

Grandpa raised his furry eyebrows. "Girls, do you need any help with your assignment?"

Shelly looked at Echo. Echo giggled. "No, we're supposed to do it on our own." And that's exactly what the friends did.

AFTER THE GIRLS HAD WORKED FOR several hours, Echo said, "I don't want to go to school tomorrow."

"But our projects are turning out great," Shelly answered. "We even found two snapping shrimp." Shelly almost wished they hadn't found the loud creatures. Their popping noises were driving her crazy.

"I'm afraid the kids will make fun of me," Echo said.

Shelly thought her friend might be right. Even though the pot was finally off Echo's tail, Rocky and Pearl did like to tease, and a pot on a tail was kind of funny. But then Shelly remembered something her grandfather had told her: "Sticks and stones may break my bones, but words will never hurt me."

"But words *do* hurt my feelings sometimes," Echo said.

"They only hurt if you let them," Shelly said. "Just pretend you don't care. If you don't get upset, everyone will stop teasing."

"Will that really work?" Echo asked.

Shelly nodded. "Of course it will." She sure hoped she was right.

Best Merfriend Ever

HEY, POT-TAIL, WHERE'S YOUR pot?" Rocky asked the next morning at school.

"Right here," Echo said, holding up the pot that now held Shelly's and Echo's projects.

Rocky grinned and said, "I liked it better on your tail."

Shelly was surprised and happy that Rocky didn't say another word. Echo had been worried for no reason.

Mrs. Karp splashed her tail sharply, and all the merstudents quickly found their desks. Shelly and Echo proudly turned in their reports, but they couldn't believe their eyes when Kiki turned in at least a dozen seaweed pages and a small chest full of shrimp and krill.

"Wow," Echo whispered. "She must be really smart."

Kiki overheard this as she sat down in her seat. She shrugged. "I'm so sorry I hit you in the stomach at practice yesterday. I felt so bad, I came back to school and worked late on my report."

"It's okay," Shelly said. "I wasn't hurt." Now *she* felt sorry. She hadn't said good-bye to Kiki when she'd left the park yesterday. Shelly hoped she hadn't hurt Kiki's feelings.

Mrs. Karp frowned when Rocky turned in two small seaweed pages with a harle-quin shrimp and Pearl handed in four shrimp that clearly had prices marked on their tails.

Pearl swam back to her seat and muttered, "My dad had to work late. He said the project was silly anyway."

Shelly had to admit she'd actually enjoyed working on the project. She'd never known there were so many different kinds of shrimp in the waters around her home.

At lunchtime, Echo and Shelly sat at a table together. Wanda and some other mergirls who boarded at Trident filled up Pearl's table. Many of them wore sparkly cloths tied around their tails.

"See what you started?" Shelly smiled. "Now *everyone's* wearing something glittery around their tails."

"How funny is that?" Echo said with

a giggle. "Maybe something even funnier would make Mr. Fangtooth smile. But what can we do?"

Shelly took a bite of her glasswort sandwich before looking around the lunchroom. She saw Kiki floating over to a small table in the corner. She was going to eat lunch all by herself. "Would you mind if we made someone else smile today?" Shelly asked Echo.

"Who?" Echo asked.

Shelly nodded toward Kiki. "She's new to Trident City, and I think she's a little lonely. Her family lives far away."

The two friends stared at Kiki. She wasn't smiling, and she looked like she'd rather be anyplace but Trident Academy.

Echo smiled. "I told you that you are the best merfriend ever. Let's go sit with her and make her feel at home."

And that's exactly what they did.

Class Reports

SNAPPING SHRIMP

By Shelly Siren

My favorite shrimp is the snapping shrimp, even though it is noisy. It's only the size of my finger, but when its jaws snap shut, it sounds like a hundred merpeople cracking their knuckles. I was lucky to find one, since they usually live in warm, shallow waters.

HARLEQUIN SHRIMP

By Echo Reef

My favorite shrimp is the harlequin shrimp. I like the blue-spotted ones the best, although the purple-, red-, and orange-spotted ones are nice too. The only thing I don't like about harlequin shrimp is that they eat starfish. I like starfish a lot, and I hate to see them hurt.

CLEANER SHRIMP

By Rocky Ridge

Cleaner shrimp are the best because they eat dead stuff out of a fish's mouth. One time I let a cleaner shrimp live in my mouth for a month. I didn't have to brush my teeth until my dad saw it and made me spit it out.

ANEMONE SHRIMP
By Pearl Swamp

I think all shrimp and krill are disgusting, but if I had to pick a favorite, I would pick the anemone shrimp. I like its purple and white spots because they look a little bit like pearls. This shrimp can live beside an anemone without getting stung.

ANTARCTIC KRILL
By Kiki Coral

I think Antarctic krill are interesting, but I am very worried about them. Because the waters are getting warmer, there are fewer krill. A single blue whale can eat as many as four million krill in a day. What will happen to the whales if the krill disappear? I think merfolk should find out what is making the waters warmer and stop it.

The Mermaid Tales Song

WORDS BY DEBBIE DADEY

REFRAIN:

Let the water roar

Deep down we're swimming along

Twirling, swirling, singing the mermaid song.

VERSE 1:

Shelly flips her tail

Racing, diving, chasing a whale

Twirling, swirling, singing the mermaid song.

VERSE 2:

Pearl likes to shine

Oh my Neptune, she looks so fine

Twirling, swirling, singing the mermaid song.

VERSE 3:

Shining Echo flips her tail

Backward and forward without fail

Twirling, swirling, singing the mermaid song.

VERSE 4:

Amazing Kiki

Far from home and floating so free

Twirling, swirling, singing the mermaid song.

Author's Note

OCEANS ARE HUGE, WILD, wonderful places that need our help. Grandpa Siren knows the dangers of oil in the ocean, and I hope you do too. We must do what we can to protect our waters from pollution.

Scientists find new creatures in the ocean all the time. Maybe one day they will find a mermaid! Check out the glossary for some interesting information about oceans and their inhabitants. Write to me on Kids Talk at www.debbiedadey.com and tell me your favorite sea creature.

Take care,
Debbie Dadey

Glossary

BLUE WHALE: The blue whale is the largest animal that has ever lived. Its heart is the size of a car!

CLAM: In real life, the giant clam is usually only five feet wide.

CLEANER SHRIMP: These shrimp clean parasites and bacteria off fish.

CONCH: Sea snail shells are sometimes used for decoration or even for blowing to make noise.

CRAB: The Japanese spider crab is the largest crab and can sometimes live for one hundred years!

CRUSTACEAN: Krill, lobsters, crabs, and shrimp are all part of a group of animals known as crustaceans.

DOGFISH: The piked dogfish is actually a shark. It can live to be one hundred years old.

DOLPHIN: The bottlenose dolphin is known to play with humans in the wild.

EMPEROR SHRIMP: Emperor shrimp live on sea cucumbers.

GLASSWORT: Common glasswort can be eaten. Sometimes it is boiled like asparagus.

GREEN SEA TURTLE: Green sea turtles lay up to two hundred eggs at a time, but their numbers still have dwindled because they are hunted for human food.

HAMMERHEAD SHARK: The strange, broad shape of this shark's head actually helps it in hunting for food.

HARLEQUIN SHRIMP: Somehow these small shrimp are able to work in pairs to catch much larger starfish.

HINGE-BEAK SHRIMP: Some shrimp actually glow!

HUMPBACK WHALE: Male humpback whale songs can be heard from miles away by other humpbacks.

JELLYFISH: The moon jellyfish is the most common of the two hundred types of jellyfish, some of which glow.

KILLER WHALE: The killer whale is not a whale at all, but a dolphin.

KRILL: Antarctic krill are only about two inches long. Krill feed on algae that grow under the ice.

OCTOPUS: The giant octopus changes color to suit its mood. If it's mad, it turns red.

ORANGE SEA PEN: This sea creature looks like an old-fashioned quill pen.

OYSTER AND MUSSEL: Oysters have long been eaten by man, and this has led the common oyster to nearly disappear. Most oysters eaten today are commercially farmed.

PAINTED STINKFISH: Painted stinkfish are colorful and like to bury themselves in the sand.

PLANKTON: Plankton is an organism that cannot swim strongly, so it flows with the currents.

RIBBON WORM: Nemertine worms, also known as "ribbon worms," can grow to be as long as a football field is wide.

SEA CUCUMBER: Sea cucumbers clean up the bottom of the sea.

SEA LILY: Sea lilies live on the seafloor and are similar in many ways to starfish.

SEAWEED: Giant kelp is the largest seaweed. It can grow two feet in one day!

SNAPPING SHRIMP: This tiny creature is only one to two inches long, but its tremendous snapping sound makes it one of the loudest animals in the ocean.

SPONGE: The Mediterranean bath sponge is soft enough to make a cushion!

STARFISH: Starfish are also known as sea stars. Most have five arms, but there is a seven-arm starfish as well as the crown-of-thorns starfish, which has up to twenty arms.

VENT TUBE WORM: Huge worms (as tall as a person) live near hot water vents on the ocean floor.

ZOOPLANKTON: This is animal plankton. Jellyfish are a type of zooplankton.

Battle of the
Best Friends

To Nixon Fow,
may you have many adventures
in your third year

★ ★ ★ ★

Acknowledgment

Thanks to my daughter, Becky Dadey,

who brings music to our shell.

1

The News

WHAT IS TAKING SHELLY so long?" Echo asked. She swam back and forth, then peeked around the corner of her shell. If Shelly didn't hurry, they would be late for school.

"Too bad I don't have one of those gadgets humans use to talk to someone who's far away," Echo said.

People fascinated Echo. Ever since Shelly's grandfather had told her about their machines that capture singing, Echo had wanted to see a human. She even wondered what it would be like to *not* have a tail.

She did a huge backward flip and smiled. Having a tail did have *some* advantages. If she kept practicing her flips, she hoped to make the Tail Flippers team at her new school, Trident Academy. Tryouts were this week. Her best friend, Shelly, had already tried out for the Shell Wars sports team at school. Echo did another flip, this time twisting sideways.

"That was great," Shelly said, swimming up beside her.

"There you are!" Echo squealed. "Have you heard the news?"

"Yes!" Shelly shouted. "I can't wait!"

"Me neither," Echo said. "Come on, let's get to school."

The two mergirls splashed past the statues of famous merfolk in MerPark.

"I can't believe Pearl was able to do it," Echo said as they swam quickly along.

Shelly brushed a lock of red hair out of her face. "Pearl?" she asked. "Pearl didn't even try out." Pearl was another mergirl in their third-grade class, who seemed to think she was better than everyone else.

Echo laughed as they reached the

entrance to their school. "You don't have to try out; you just need lots of jewels to pay for them."

"You can *pay* to get on the Shell Wars team?" Shelly asked. "I thought Pearl hated Shell Wars."

Echo stopped and stared at her friend. "*What* are you talking about?"

"I'm talking about Shell Wars. Coach Barnacle announces who made the team today. What are *you* talking about?"

Echo grabbed Shelly's hands and squeezed them tightly. "I'm talking about Pearl's birthday party. She's invited the Rays!"

"You're kidding!" Shelly screamed. There wasn't a merperson alive who hadn't heard of the Rays. They were an amazing boy band and they were very, very cute.

"Didn't you get your invitation?" Echo asked.

Shelly shook her head.

"I bet you'll get it today," Echo told her friend. She smiled as they went into the school, but she was a little worried. Pearl wasn't exactly the nicest mergirl in their class, and she didn't like Shelly very much.

What if Pearl hadn't invited Shelly? What would Echo do?

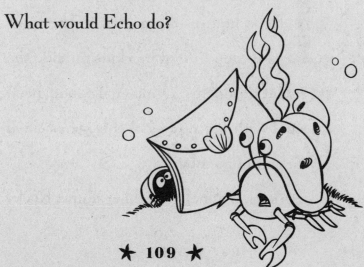

Pearl

I MADE IT!" SHELLY YELLED. SHE AND
Echo had finally gotten to the front
of a long line of merkids outside the
Trident Academy gym. A list had been
posted with the names of this year's Shell
Wars team members.

As soon as Shelly read her name, Rocky

pushed her out of the way. "Move it!" said the merboy, who was in Shelly and Echo's class. "If you made the team, I had to make it too. You stink!"

Echo and Shelly backed away from the list to let the crowd behind them see. Everyone wanted to know who had made their grade's team.

"Congratulations," said Kiki. She was a small, dark-haired mergirl new to Trident City and a new friend of Shelly's.

"You'll be the best Shell Wars player ever," Echo added.

Shelly laughed. "I'd just be happy not getting smacked in the stomach with the shell. But, Kiki, I'm so sorry you didn't make the team."

★ 111 ★

Kiki shrugged. "It's okay. I've never really played it before, so I knew it was a long shot. I'll join some clubs instead."

"There are some amazing clubs here at Trident Academy," Echo said.

Shelly nodded. "I can't believe our first Shell Wars game is Thursday."

Echo gasped. "That's when the Tail Flippers tryouts are! I wanted to go to your first game."

"I wanted to watch *you* try out," Shelly said. "Maybe I can come during halftime."

"I'll watch," Kiki said, "and cheer for Echo. Next time I'll go to your game, Shelly."

"Thanks," Shelly said. "Echo, I know you'll make the team."

"Right now we'd better get to class," Echo said as the conch shell horn began to sound. All the kids in the hall raced to their classrooms. Echo, Kiki, and Shelly slid into their rock desks just as the final sound blasted. Rocky, who was always late, swam in seconds later.

Pearl was already in class. Echo wanted to ask her about the party. Maybe she hadn't sent out all her invitations yet. Maybe Shelly's got lost in the underwater snail mail. Maybe Pearl didn't know Shelly's address.

Echo was so worried about Shelly and the party, she didn't hear a word anyone said until her teacher, Mrs. Karp, announced, "The report is due on Monday."

Monday? I'll just have to find out later what the assignment is, Echo thought. *I need to speak to Pearl before I do anything!*

Echo finally got the chance to ask Pearl about the party after school at Tail Flippers practice.

"I'll see Shelly later if you want me to give her the invitation," Shelly told Pearl.

"No thanks," Pearl said, gently removing the long strand of pearls she wore around her neck and putting it on a nearby rock. No jewelry was allowed during any after-school sports. "I don't invite icky Shell Wars players to my lovely home."

"But you invited Rocky," Echo said. She had heard Rocky talking about the party in the lunchroom.

Pearl giggled. "I know. He's *so* cute, and we need boys for dancing."

"But Shelly is really nice. You'll find out when you get to know her better," Echo said.

"I know all I want to know," Pearl said with a sniff. "And from now on, if you want to be friends with me, you can't be friends with Shelly."

Awful

I CAN'T BELIEVE PEARL!" SAID SHELLY the next morning while the girls made their way to school. "Did she really say that?"

Echo nodded sadly. "I told her to take her friendship and feed it to the sea turtles."

Shelly hugged her friend. "Thanks for

sticking up for me," she said. "But I know you've always wanted to see the Rays. You've taught me all of their songs."

Echo laughed. "I bet you sing better than they do." Echo had to admit she was a little bit jealous of Shelly's singing. Every mergirl could sing well, but some had a special gift and sang like sirens of long ago. Shelly had that gift.

"Maybe we should have our own party," Shelly said as the girls swam past MerPark. "We could have a Rays sing-along of our own for everyone who wasn't invited. Kiki told me she didn't get an invitation either."

Echo splashed up and down. "Great idea, Shelly!"

"We *could* do that, but I still think you should go to Pearl's party. I don't have to do everything you do," Shelly said.

"I know," Echo said. "But if I go, it's like I agree with Pearl, and I don't. She shouldn't be so mean."

"But this is the chance of a lifetime," Shelly argued.

Echo shrugged. "Mergirls live very long lives, so I'm sure I'll get another chance to see the Rays."

Shelly didn't say anything. She just nodded.

Zoom! Something rushed past the girls and into Trident Academy.

"What was that?" Echo asked. "It wasn't a shark, was it?" The residents of Trident

City were always on the lookout for sharks. Even though they rarely came into waters this deep, the city had shark patrols that kept constant watch.

"That wasn't a shark," Shelly said. "It was Rocky."

"I can't help it," Echo said with a giggle. "I still think he's awfully cute."

"He's awful, all right," Shelly said, remembering the time he swiped a shrimp she was getting for a project, "but I'm not sure about the cute part."

Upside-Down Day

DID YOU WORK ON YOUR famous merperson report?" Shelly asked Echo as they entered the enormous front hallway of Trident Academy. All around them, hundreds of merkids chatted with their friends. A couple of merboys tossed a lemon sponge back and forth until Coach Barnacle told them to stop.

"What report?" Echo said, swimming around a group of giggling tenth-grade mergirls.

"Didn't you hear Mrs. Karp tell us to do a report on a merperson?"

"When did she say that?" Echo asked. She shook her head and ducked when a fourth grader swam over her in a rush to get to class.

Shelly stopped swimming. "Wait a minute," she said. She took a deep breath and faced Echo. "I am working very hard to do my best at Trident. After all, it's a family tradition. My parents and grand-parents all went to school here. It's really,

really important that I do well."

"I know," Echo said. "Don't worry. You'll do great."

Shelly scrunched her nose up. She looked right at Echo and said, "I can't be friends with someone who doesn't even *try* in school."

Echo fell backward in surprise. "What?"

"You heard me," Shelly said. "I thought about it all night, and it's best if we're not friends anymore." And then she swam away.

Echo couldn't believe her ears. *What happened?* How could Shelly treat her this way? They had been best friends for as long as she could remember.

ALL MORNING LONG, SHELLY IGNORED Echo during class. At lunch, Shelly turned her back on Echo and sat at a table for two with Kiki.

"Come sit with us," Pearl said, pulling Echo's pink tail.

Echo sat with Pearl and her friends, but she didn't say a word. Instead, she watched Shelly and Kiki. They looked like they were having a great time without her, talking and laughing. They even walked on their hands in front of Mr. Fangtooth, the cafeteria worker.

"They are trying to make him laugh," Echo said, breaking her silence.

Pearl looked at Mr. Fangtooth. "He's such a grouch. They'll never cheer him up. How ridiculous!"

Echo didn't think it was silly to be nice. In fact, she thought it was the best thing in the world. And more than anything, she wanted to make Mr. Fangtooth laugh with Shelly and Kiki. On the first day

of third grade the mergirls had made crabby-looking Mr. Fangtooth laugh. Even though they had gotten into trouble, they were glad they'd tried to make him happy.

Echo stood up. Shelly looked at her. Immediately Shelly and Kiki rushed back to their table and sat down. Echo couldn't help herself—she quickly swam out of the cafeteria. Then, in the hallway, she cried and cried.

Tryouts

THIS IS SO THRILLING!" PEARL squealed as twenty mergirls lined up for the Tail Flippers tryouts on Thursday. The MerPark stands were full of friends and family who had come to watch the after-school event.

Echo knew she should be excited. After all, she had practiced ever since the first day of school. Her father and mother had taken off work to see her try out. Her older sister, Crystal, even came to watch. Kiki was in the stands supporting her. But all Echo could think about was the way Shelly had treated her. It was the worst time of her life.

Echo was beginning to think that Trident Academy was bad for their friendship. At the beginning of the school year, she and Shelly had an argument about homework. They never used to argue. "I should just go home now," Echo said out loud. "I'm never going to make the team."

Wanda, a mergirl in Echo's class and

Kiki's roommate, frowned. "You'll never make it with that attitude. You have to be confident, Echo."

Echo sighed. She wasn't confident at all. She was way too sad. She missed her friend. But then she heard something that changed everything.

"Good luck, Echo!" someone shouted. Echo looked up in the stands and saw Kiki. And right beside her, *Shelly* held a big seaweed sign that read GO ECHO! in red letters.

Great! Shelly must not be mad anymore, Echo thought, and waved at her friends.

"All right, merladies," announced Coach Barnacle. "Let the tryouts begin."

The Trident Academy Pep Band played

their instruments. Several older mer-students used conch shells to blow tunes while three merboys pounded out a beat on a huge sharkskin drum. Suddenly Coach Barnacle smashed two shells together. "That's our signal," Pearl said.

All twenty mergirls began flipping backward and sideways to the music. The merpeople in the stands clapped along. Echo giggled. It was so much fun. She was doing her best turns and flips. She was happy, but mostly because Shelly was there to support her.

The music stopped and Coach Barnacle chose five girls from the group: Pearl, Echo, and three others Echo didn't know. Echo felt bad for Wanda and the girls who weren't chosen. They had worked just as hard as she had.

"Congratulations! You are the new Tail Flippers team!" Coach said. "We start practice tomorrow after school, so don't be late. See you then."

Echo swam over to her parents and her sister.

"Your flips were fantastic," Crystal said.

"Did you really think so?" Echo asked.

"You'll be a wonderful member of the team," Echo's mother added. "Your father and I have to get back to work, but we'll celebrate at home later."

Echo's family left, and she found Kiki. "Thanks so much for coming," Echo said, hugging her. "Where is Shelly?"

"Who?" Kiki asked.

"I saw Shelly right beside you," Echo said. "I wanted to ask her about her game."

Kiki shrugged. "I heard they won, but I think she's still mad at you."

The smile on Echo's face disappeared. "But she was holding up a good-luck sign. I thought she wasn't angry anymore. Why would she come to cheer me on? Oh, Kiki, how can Shelly and I be friends again?"

Kiki looked down at the sandy ocean floor and twitched her purple tail. "I don't know," she said softly.

All Echo wanted to do was go home and cry. She didn't even care that she had made the Tail Flippers team.

"Bye," Echo said sadly as she floated away from MerPark.

"I'm sorry," Kiki called after her.

I'm sorry too, Echo said to herself. *Why couldn't I have paid attention in class? Then none of this would have happened.*

A soft hand grabbed Echo's arm. "Isn't it totally fabulous?" Pearl asked. "We made the Tail Flippers!"

Echo nodded. "Yeah, it's great."

"You have to come to my house to celebrate," Pearl said. "My mom will make us coconut shakes."

"What's a coconut?" Echo asked.

Pearl laughed. "It's food that humans eat. It looks like a big, round ball and grows on this thing called a tree on land.

Sometimes the coconuts fall into the ocean. They are very rare and quite delicious."

Echo shook her head. "Thanks, but . . ."

Pearl wouldn't take no for an answer. "You have to come. We can celebrate and work on our famous merperson assignment for Monday. We have a whole merlibrary filled with lots of stories. And I'll tell you all about my party!"

Echo was so upset about losing Shelly as a friend that she decided to go with Pearl. "All right," Echo said halfheartedly. After all, she did need to do her report.

PEARL LIVED IN THE BIGGEST HOME IN Shell Estates. It was almost as big as Trident Academy. Her shell's ceiling was

lined with hundreds of different-colored jellyfish lamps. A spectacular seaweed curtain hung beside a curving marble staircase. The curtain and staircase were encrusted with thousands of gleaming jewels.

"Your home is beautiful," Echo said.

"I know," Pearl said. "We might get a bigger one next year."

As the mergirls swam into a massive rock library, Echo couldn't imagine anyone needing a bigger shell. Pearl's home *was* nice, but the only place Echo wanted to be was with Shelly at the apartment she shared with her grandfather above the People Museum.

Echo wondered if she'd ever get the chance to be there again.

6

Kiki's Secret

EVERYONE'S TAILS ARE GLEAMING," Pearl said to Echo the next day at lunch. "I told them they had to polish themselves if they wanted to come to my party tonight."

Echo glanced at her own tail. It was looking a bit dull. "I'll shine mine later."

Pearl looked down her pointy nose at Echo. "Well, I should hope so. It's too bad we have Tail Flippers practice after school. I wonder if Coach Barnacle would excuse me since it's my birthday."

Echo shrugged. "It is our first official practice."

Pearl rolled her eyes. "I know. We can't miss it or we'll get kicked off the team. Maybe I shouldn't have even tried out! What's more important than my birthday?" She swam away to buy her lunch. She had told Echo she always chose the black-lip oyster and sablefish stew because it was the most expensive item on the menu.

Echo sighed and looked down at her hagfish jelly sandwich. She wasn't hungry, but merpeople never wasted food. It was too precious. So she slowly chewed every last bite. She was surprised that Pearl hadn't come back to their table yet. When Echo looked around, she saw Pearl sticking her tongue out at Mr. Fangtooth. But she wasn't doing it to make him laugh, she was doing it to be cruel.

Echo jumped up from the table. She had to stop Pearl from being so mean! She started to rush over to Mr. Fangtooth when—*slam!*—she collided with Kiki, right in the middle of the lunchroom. Everyone stopped eating and stared at them. Rocky and a few other boys laughed.

"Mergirl sea wreck," Rocky joked.

Echo's cheeks turned red.

"I'm sorry," Kiki told Echo.

"Me too," Echo said. "I didn't see you coming."

"I need to tell you something now, while Shelly is in the art room," Kiki said softly. "She's working on a special project, and I have to go help her. I should have told you this yesterday, but Shelly doesn't want you to know."

Echo put her right hand on her hip. "I already know what you're going to say: Shelly is *still* mad at me."

Kiki shook her head. "No, Echo. Shelly isn't mad at all."

"Yes, she is. She's been mean to me all week. She hasn't spoken to me once," Echo said.

"Shelly is only *pretending* to be angry," Kiki said. "She knows you want to see the Rays at Pearl's party. But you're such a good friend, you won't go unless she's invited too. Don't tell her I told you! After today—when the party is over—she'll try to be friends again. I hope you'll let her."

Kiki swam away and Echo was left with her mouth open in surprise. Was Kiki telling the truth?

Non-Rays Party

ECHO WAS DYING TO TALK TO Shelly during class, but Mrs. Karp kept them too busy all afternoon. After school Shelly was nowhere to be found, and Echo had Tail Flippers practice.

"Oh my Neptune!" Pearl said at MerPark. "Just think, in a few short hours we are actually going to see the Rays—all because of me!"

The other girls on the team squealed in delight, but Echo just smiled. She had to admit, it was pretty amazing that such a famous group would be in Trident City.

It was hard for the team to concentrate on practice. Pearl forgot to take off her necklace and got her tail tangled up. It took the first half of practice just to unsnarl her. Then Pearl's and Echo's tails collided and they both crashed to the ocean floor.

Finally Coach Barnacle gave up, threw his hands in the air, and said, "Girls, go

home. Hopefully we'll have better luck at the next practice."

"Yes!" shouted Pearl. "I'm going home to put on my new outfit."

"Bye!" Echo said, zooming off as fast as she could. She didn't head home to polish the scales on her tail. She didn't head home to change into party clothes. She swam right past her shell to Shelly's apartment at the People Museum.

"Watch it!" snapped an old merwoman, who was moving slowly toward Manta Ray Station.

"Sorry," Echo called, zipping around the merlady and her wolffish.

"Merkids think they own the entire ocean," the merwoman muttered. The startled wolffish hid behind a rock until the old merwoman coaxed it out.

Echo found Shelly in her room, resting on a bath sponge. "Congratulations on winning your first Shell Wars game," Echo said. "I'm sorry I didn't get to see it, but I did make the Tail Flippers team. I saw you cheering for me in the stands."

"Echo!" Shelly screamed. "What are you doing here? Why aren't you at Pearl's shell?"

"Because I want to be with a *real* friend," Echo said.

"But . . . I'm not your friend. Not anymore," Shelly said slowly.

Echo laughed. "I know better. You were only pretending to be mad so I would go to the party."

Shelly's face turned red. "How did you find out? Did Kiki tell you?"

"Don't blame Kiki," Echo said. "You are more important to me than any silly band."

"But I know you wanted to see the Rays. That's why I made up the story about you not trying hard enough in class," Shelly said.

"But I'd rather be your friend than see any boy band," Echo said.

Shelly hugged Echo. "Are you sure?"

"I'm sure." Echo knew she was doing the right thing. "Let's go to the Big Rock Café for a colossal kelp drink," Echo said. "We can celebrate your Shell Wars victory and my making the Tail Flippers."

"The two of us can celebrate another

day. Right now it's time for the party at the Big Rock Café."

"You decided to have the sing-along anyway?" Echo asked.

"Yes," Shelly explained. "Kiki and I made signs to let everyone who wasn't invited to Pearl's party know about our celebration at the Big Rock."

"So that's what you were doing in the art room when I was talking to Kiki. What a good idea," Echo said.

"Let's go!" Shelly said. The two girls sped off to the café. When they swam in the doorway, they couldn't believe their eyes!

Great Wasp Tragedy

SITTING AT THE ROCK COUNTER were the Rays. All four of them! Hanging above them was a sign that said WHO NEEDS THE RAYS? LET'S MAKE OUR OWN MUSIC! Everyone in the Big Rock Café stared at the boy band, even the merwaitresses and mercooks.

Kiki rushed over to Shelly and Echo. "I thought this was a party *without* the Rays. How did you get the most famous band in the ocean to come here?"

Echo held up her palms in surprise. Shelly shrugged and said, "We didn't do anything, but there's one way to find out."

"You're going to talk to them?" Kiki asked, barely whispering.

"Of course. They're only merpeople," Shelly said.

"But they're stars," Echo whimpered. "They probably don't even *speak* to ordinary mergirls like us."

"Well, if they don't, it will be a short

conversation," Shelly said, pulling Echo toward the Rays. Kiki swam along, hiding behind Echo.

"Excuse me," Shelly said. "I'm Shelly. These are my friends Echo and Kiki. It's cool you're here, but aren't you supposed to be at Pearl's party?"

A handsome merboy not much older than Shelly leaped off his rock stool. "Greetings, merladies. Lovely to meet you. I'm Alden, and this is Harmon," he said in a strange accent. "You're right. We are supposed to be at a party, but there's a problem."

Harmon, an even cuter merboy, put a hand on Alden's shoulder. "Our backup singer was stung by a sea wasp today. It was horrible."

"Oh no!" Kiki said, sticking her head

out from behind Echo. "Sea wasps are so

poisonous. Is your singer okay?"

Alden shook his head. "Doc Weedly says Gwen will be better in a week. But she can't sing a bubble until she gets well." Alden pointed to two other band members. "Teddy and Ellis sing, but we still need a mergirl's voice."

"I'm so sorry about your singer," Echo said to the band. She couldn't believe she was having a conversation with Alden of the Rays!

"We'd like to honor our commitment to Pearl, but we can't go on without Gwen, even though she wants us to," Alden told them.

Shelly nodded. "It's too bad. Pearl is going to be terribly disappointed. You're all she's been talking about this week."

Echo couldn't believe her ears. After all, Pearl hadn't even invited Shelly to the party. But then Echo had an idea. It was a totally fabulous, crazy idea.

"You know," Echo said, "I know someone who is a super singer. And she knows every word to every one of your songs."

"Really? Who is it? Where is she?" the Rays said together.

Echo put her arm around Shelly's shoulders and said, "She's right here. It's Shelly!"

Shelly jerked away from Echo. "Are you shell-shocked? I can't do that!"

Alden grabbed Shelly's hand and said, "Why not? Let's do it. It will be a blast!"

Shelly backed away. "No way! I can't go to Pearl's party. I wasn't invited."

Teddy piped up, "You're invited now. You're part of the band."

"But I'm having a sing-along here for my friends," Shelly explained,

NON-RAYS PARTY

pointing to the sign above their heads. "I can't leave them behind." The Rays looked around the Big Rock Café. Kiki and then other kids waved shyly at the band.

"Sorry about the sign. We really do like you," Kiki explained.

The Rays looked above them and grinned at the words WHO NEEDS THE RAYS?

"Guess what?" Alden said to the kids in the café. "You're all coming to Pearl's party as our guests. We'll rock together. Are you with us?"

Pearl's Party Crashers

I CAN'T BELIEVE IT! YOU'RE REALLY here!" Pearl shrieked when she saw the Rays. "Please come in," she said, pointing the way inside her grand shell.

"Great," Alden said. "We hope you don't mind that we brought a few friends of ours too."

Pearl giggled. "Any friends of yours are welcome."

"Totally cool. Come on, guys." The four Rays stood by as Shelly, Kiki, Echo, and all the kids from the Big Rock Café floated toward Pearl's home. Pearl's mouth dropped open when she saw who was with the band.

"You aren't invited to this party," Pearl snapped at Shelly, and blocked the entrance to her home.

"She's part of the band," Alden explained, swimming up beside Shelly. "Our backup singer was stung by a sea wasp, and Shelly is helping us out."

Harmon piped up, "Of course, we'd understand if you'd rather we cancel. We have had a very hard day."

"Oh no, you can't cancel," Pearl said quickly. Pearl frowned at Shelly, but moved out of the way. "Everyone can come on in."

In a few short minutes the Rays had set up their instruments on the huge marble staircase in Pearl's entryway.

"Are you sure I can do this?" Shelly asked Echo.

Echo hugged her friend. "I know you can."

Shelly took a deep breath and swam between Alden, Harmon, Teddy, and Ellis.

"Shark, the sharpnose sevengill, lived near to me. We swam together every day and became

the best of friends," Teddy sang, and all the girls in the audience screamed, even Kiki and Echo.

"Best of friends," sang Shelly.

"Go, Shelly!" yelled Echo.

"Then someone told Shark he should eat me. And now I miss him terribly," sang Teddy. *"But our friendship had to end."*

"Had to end," sang Shelly.

"Shark, the sharpnose sevengill, lived near to me," sang Ellis. *"I'll always treasure our friendship. And hope someday he'll see . . ."*

Then Teddy and Ellis leaned together and motioned for Shelly to join them. *"That sharks and merfolks can be friends. One day it will be."*

Shelly repeated, *"One day it will be."*

Then the Rays and Shelly finished the song. *"But until that day I guess I'll say, 'Shark, I miss you still.'"*

"I miss you still!" Shelly sang in the most amazing high voice.

Kiki grinned as everyone cheered. "Shelly is really good."

Echo nodded. She knew Shelly would be.

When the song ended, all the merkids clapped wildly. Then Alden pointed to Pearl.

"Happy birthday to Pearl. We want to thank you for inviting us."

"Thank Shelly!" Kiki yelled. "Without her, there'd be no show."

Alden laughed. "That's right. Let's hear it for Shelly." Everyone cheered as Shelly waved and the Rays started a new song.

"Do you think Pearl will be mad you said that?" Echo asked Kiki.

Kiki shook her head. "Any other mergirl would thank Shelly for helping. Without her, the party would have been canceled."

"Pearl's not like anyone else. That's for sure," Echo whispered to Kiki. "Look."

Echo pointed to Pearl. Pearl wasn't cheering. And she wasn't singing along to the music. She was glaring right at Shelly.

Star

SHELLY, YOU'RE A STAR!" WANDA told Shelly at school on Monday. Shelly's face turned bright red. "It was a lot of fun, but I was so afraid I'd mess up."

"It was the most amazing party ever," Kiki added. "I didn't want the Rays to leave."

Shelly nodded. "They were so nice."

"You mean you actually got to talk to them?" another mergirl asked. Almost every merkid in class gathered around Shelly.

Shelly nodded. "Echo, Kiki, and I all did."

Pearl sniffed. "I talked to them too," she said.

"Alden is *sooooo* cute," a girl named Morgan whispered.

Echo giggled. "He even held Shelly's hand." Several girls almost fainted, so it was a good thing Mrs. Karp swooped into the room. "Class, please turn in your merperson assignments."

Everyone except for Rocky passed in his or her report.

"Rocky, where is yours?" asked Mrs. Karp.

Rocky shrugged. "A killer whale stole it from me on the way to school."

Mrs. Karp nodded and said, "Tomorrow you may turn in your merperson report as well as one on killer whales."

Rocky slouched down in his chair while Mrs. Karp glanced over the seaweed pages. "Hmm, this is strange. Pearl's and Echo's stories begin the exact same way."

Echo gasped and looked at Pearl. Did Pearl copy her report when they'd worked at her house? Pearl turned red and looked down at her desk. She played with her long necklace and wouldn't look at Echo. Thankfully, Mrs. Karp didn't say anything else about the stories and pointed to a big chart on the wall showing different kinds of whales.

Later at lunch, Pearl swam over to Shelly and said, "You're a star all because of me and my party! Why don't you sit at *my* table today?"

Echo couldn't believe Pearl! She was so angry with her. Pearl not only copied her story, now she was trying to take away Echo's friend. Would Shelly go with Pearl?

"Thanks," Shelly said, "but Kiki and Echo liked me even when I didn't sing with the Rays, so I'll sit with them."

"Suit yourself," Pearl snapped. "Sit with those bottom-feeders."

"They aren't bottom-feeders," Shelly

said. "Kiki and Echo are amazing mergirls, and if it wasn't for them, the Rays wouldn't have been at your party. Echo's idea saved the day."

Pearl stuck her nose up in the air. "Humph," she said, before rushing off to her table.

"She makes me mad enough to scream," Shelly said.

"Don't scream, Shelly." Echo giggled. "You'll ruin your voice!"

Echo pulled Shelly toward another table. "And don't worry about Pearl," Echo said. "The three of us are best friends, and that makes us winners."

Kiki nodded. "Winners every time."

Class Reports

★ ✦ ★

**THE STORY OF
MARIS**

By Shelly Siren

Maris ruled the
sea many years ago, when Trident City
was first built. She rode a killer whale and
traveled freely among the many merpeople
and ocean animals. Not only was she
kind and fair, but she made peace with the

sharks by offering them their own hunting grounds. Once she was challenged by an evil merman who lunged at her with a sharp whalebone. She called out to all her animal friends for help. In a flash, the evil merman was eaten by a shark. Maris recovered and ruled for many more years.

THE STORY OF ALANNA

By Echo Reef

Alanna lived in ancient times, before Trident City was even built. She had a beautiful voice and often tricked human sailors into following her. One sailor happened to see her when his ship sank. He fell in love with her. Alanna saved him, but after that she never teased sailors again. It is believed she fell in love with the sailor, and that is what made her seek to pass the merfolk law to never taunt human sailors.

THE STORY OF MERLIN

By Rocky Ridge

Merlin may or may not have been a merperson. He lived with the merfolk for many years and showed them much magic. He may have used his magic to become a merman. Magic means making something extraordinary happen. Merlin could wave a wand when he was hungry and make a school of fish appear. He could talk with sharks and is believed to be the only merman to ever ride a great white.

MY REPORT ON KILLER WHALES
By Rocky Ridge

Killer whales do not normally eat seaweed school reports, but it is possible. Usually they eat fish, squid, birds, seals, and even other whales. They are big and black and white.

THE STORY OF ALANNA

By Pearl Swamp

I HAD TO DO IT OVER!

Many years ago, before Trident City was even built, there was a beautiful mermaid named Alanna. Everything about her was beautiful, even her voice, and she liked to tease human sailors into following her. One sailor happened to see her when he fell out of his ship. He loved her. Alanna saved him, but after that she never teased sailors again. She fell in love with the sailor and that is what made her pass a law to never taunt human sailors, which, if you ask me, is a stupid law. And why would any mermaid fall in love with a human? I mean, humans don't even have tails! EWWW!

THE STORY OF MAPELLA

By Kiki Coral

Thousands of years ago near the South China Sea, a young mermaid named Mapella was born. Mapella traveled more than any merperson before her had ever dared. She loved seeing new places, but she also carved maps of everywhere she went. In the ancient mercity of Dao-Ming, visitors can still see the reliefs Mapella made. She was the first mapmaker, or cartographer, of the merpeople. She gave her name to the maps we still use today. Her traveling stopped when she was eaten by a tiger shark.

The Mermaid Song

REFRAIN:

Let the water roar

Deep down we're swimming along

Twirling, swirling, singing the mermaid song.

VERSE 1:

Shelly flips her tail

Racing, diving, chasing a whale

Twirling, swirling, singing the mermaid song.

VERSE 2:

Pearl likes to shine

Oh my Neptune, she looks so fine

Twirling, swirling, singing the mermaid song.

VERSE 3:

Shining Echo flips her tail

Backward and forward without fail

Twirling, swirling, singing the mermaid song.

VERSE 4:

Amazing Kiki

Far from home and floating so free

Twirling, swirling, singing the mermaid song.

Shark, the Sharpnose Sevengill

Shark, the sharpnose sevengill,

lived near to me

We swam together every day

and became the best of friends

Then someone told Shark

he should eat me

And now I miss him terribly

But our friendship had to end

Shark, the sharpnose sevengill,

lived near to me

I'll always treasure our friendship

And hope someday he'll see

That sharks and merfolks can be friends

One day it will be

But until that day I guess I'll say,

"Shark, I miss you still."

Author's Note

THE OCEAN IS AN AMAZING place full of secrets. There are many places underwater that have yet to be investigated by humans. Maybe one day, explorers will find a mermaid band deep on the ocean floor. Read the next pages to find out about some other amazing ocean life. I hope you'll let me know your favorite creature. You can write to me on Kids Talk at www.debbiedadey.com.

Swim free,

Debbie Dadey

Glossary

BARNACLE: A barnacle is a crustacean that sticks itself to boats or other creatures, like whales.

BATH SPONGE: The Mediterranean bath sponge is not common today because in the past, huge numbers were caught by humans and used for cleaning and bathing.

BLACK-LIP OYSTER: The black-lip pearl oyster begins life as a male and changes into a female! It sometimes produces black pearls.

COCONUT: The coconut grows on palm trees in warm climates on land. The coconut, shaped like a big brown soccer ball, has been known to get caught in ocean currents and travel great distances. It will float and it is waterproof. The inside of a coconut contains sweet liquid.

CORAL: Coral polyps are small, soft-bodied creatures that are related to jellyfish. Coral makes reefs by attaching itself to rocks and dividing. Some of the coral reefs on earth began growing fifty million years ago.

CONCH SHELL: Conch are a kind of marine mollusk that have a heavy spiral shell. In the past, jewelry makers used the shells to carve cameos.

GREAT WHITE SHARK: The great white shark is very smart and can grow up to twenty-four feet, as long as a telephone pole is tall.

HAGFISH: This long, eel-like fish can actually tie itself into knots. It does so quite often, in fact, to help it get rid of the slime that comes out of its pores.

KILLER WHALES: Killer whales (or orcas) are not whales at all, but dolphins. They live together in pods of about twenty for their entire life.

LEMON SEA SPONGE: This bright yellow sponge grows in shallow waters of the Pacific Ocean.

MANTA RAY: They are the largest rays in the ocean, and they are related to sharks. But they are not dangerous—they don't have a stinging spine.

SABLEFISH: Adult sablefish are found in deep waters and sometimes live to be ninety years old!

SEA TURTLES: Sea turtles have been on the earth for 120 million years! Leatherback sea turtles can weigh more than two thousand pounds.

SEA WASP: The sea wasp is another name for the box jellyfish, which is the world's most venomous marine animal. It lives near Australia.

SHARPNOSE SEVENGILL SHARK: This shark is on the endangered species list and lives in deep water. It usually eats squid, crustaceans, and fish near seabeds.

TIGER SHARK: The tiger shark is the second most dangerous shark to humans, after the great white. Tiger sharks will eat almost anything, even garbage. They like coastal waters.

WOLFFISH: This creepy-looking fish is usually found near rocky reefs in deep water. It grows new teeth every year.

A Whale of a Tale

To my nephew Damon Gibson,
who swam with humpback whales
and was kind enough
to tell me about it

★ ★ ★ ★

Acknowledgment

Thank you to my husband, Eric Dadey, for

putting up with me for twenty-nine years

of marriage.

Ocean Trip

ROCKY RIDGE WASN'T HAPPY. "Do we have to do another project?" he whined to his teacher. "Mrs. Karp, that's not fair!"

In the first few weeks of the new school year at Trident Academy, Mrs. Karp's third-grade class had already completed reports on famous merpeople and a project where they'd collected krill and shrimp. Every one of the twenty students hoped they wouldn't have to do another big assignment.

Mrs. Karp smiled. "This lesson is different. We're going on an ocean trip."

Rocky and the rest of the class cheered. "Yes! Awesome!"

Kiki Coral gasped. But her mergirl friends Echo Reef and Shelly Siren clapped their hands and swished their tails. For many in the class, this would be their first ocean trip. They would leave classwork behind to learn in a deep-sea environment. "It's about time we did something fun," a mergirl named Pearl Swamp snapped.

"Where are we going, Mrs. Karp?" Kiki asked.

"An article in the *Trident City Tide* reported that a pod of whales is expected to be directly above Trident City tomorrow

morning. We will visit them. In fact, Dr. Evan Mousteau will join us in a few minutes to tell us about whales and even teach us a bit of whale language."

Mrs. Karp continued, "I expect you to be courteous to Dr. Mousteau. After he leaves, we'll go over surface safety rules. Your parents can feel secure that the guards from the Shark Patrol will be on the alert all morning, not only for sharks, but also for any sign of humans."

Echo could barely speak. "Humans!" she whispered to Shelly and Kiki. "I've always wanted to see a real, live human. Maybe tomorrow will be my chance!" Everything about humans fascinated Echo.

"Are you sure it's safe? My parents

have never let me go above water," Echo said to Mrs. Karp.

Mrs. Karp patted Echo on the shoulder. "Don't worry, we will only go if it is safe."

Then Kiki shyly asked, "Which whale dialect will we be learning?"

Mrs. Karp raised her green eyebrows. "Excellent question. I wonder how many of you know that whales talk to one another?"

No one raised their hand except Shelly. Kiki smiled at her.

"Since the visiting pod is made up of humpbacks, we will focus on the humpback whale dialect," Mrs. Karp told the class.

Kiki nodded, still smiling, but in truth she was worried. Really worried.

2

Dr. Mousteau

DR. MOUSTEAU REMINDED Kiki of the bottlenose dolphins that lived near her home in the far-off waters by Asia. He had the same shiny bald head and long pointed nose. Even his eyes were round and black. Kiki wondered if Dr. Mousteau had twenty-five pairs of teeth in each jaw. When he opened his mouth, she got her answer: He had one big tooth in the center of his top gum. That was it.

"The humpback whale is a wondrous creature," Dr. Mousteau told the third graders. "The pattern of white markings on the flukes and flippers is different on each and every whale. So no two whales are alike."

Dr. Mousteau continued, "Adult humpbacks are quite large and weigh ten times more than a great white shark."

"Those whales need to go on a diet," Rocky blurted out.

Mrs. Karp frowned, but Dr. Mousteau didn't seem to mind Rocky's interruption.

He went on, "As you might know, man is the only predator of whales. Thankfully, humans' captures of whales in recent years have decreased. Still, the humpback population is about one-fifth of what it was hundreds of years ago."

Dr. Mousteau reached into a bag and took out a thick piece of skin. "I'd like each of you to touch the specimen I'm passing around. This was taken from a whale that died naturally. I brought it for you to study."

Dr. Mousteau gave the skin to Rocky, who felt and even sniffed it. Rocky tried to give it to Pearl, but she shook her head. "I don't want to touch any disgusting dead whale. It has awful bumps and nasty barnacles on it."

"That's quite normal," Dr. Mousteau said, taking the specimen and handing it to Shelly. "Every humpback has a long head with knobs such as these. If you didn't clean yourselves thoroughly, you'd have barnacles too."

"I had a barnacle one time," Rocky said, "but my dad made me wash it off."

Shelly felt the whale skin and tried to give it to Kiki, but Kiki's eyes were glued to Dr. Mousteau. "Here, Kiki," Shelly said, but Kiki wouldn't look.

Shelly shrugged and passed the skin to Echo, who took it with two fingers and quickly gave it to a mergirl named Morgan. Morgan only looked at it for a second before handing it to a merboy named Adam.

Kiki shuddered. She'd almost had to touch the whale skin. She hoped that wouldn't happen again. She tried to concentrate on Dr. Mousteau's lessons on water pressure and whale speech, even though she spoke humpback perfectly. Pearl and Echo giggled as they tried to imitate the strange sounds. Rocky sounded more like a sick seal than a whale. Shelly was surprisingly good.

After the language lesson, Dr. Mousteau said, "If you are very lucky tomorrow, three things might happen."

"What are they?" Pearl asked. "I want to be lucky."

Dr. Mousteau smiled, showing the one tooth in the middle of his mouth. "First, you may see a whale jumping out of the water."

"That's known as breaching," added Mrs. Karp.

"Cool," Rocky said.

"Number two," Dr. Mousteau said, "you may hear the males sing."

"Do the females sing?" Shelly asked.

"No," Dr. Mousteau said.

"That's not fair. Why not?" Shelly asked.

Mrs. Karp explained, "The males sing to attract females."

Dr. Mousteau nodded in agreement before continuing. "And three, if you are very lucky, you may see a baby whale."

Echo looked at Kiki. "Wouldn't that be great? Babies are so cute."

Kiki swallowed hard. "Sure," she said. But Kiki didn't think baby whales would be cute at all. In fact, whales of any size absolutely terrified her.

3

Funny Noises

THIS IS AWESOME," ECHO TOLD Kiki and Shelly in the Trident Academy lunchroom that afternoon.

Kiki looked up from her lunch of polka-dot batfish sushi in surprise. "What do you mean? This is the worst sushi they've served all year."

"I'm not talking about the food, Kiki," Echo said. "I mean the ocean trip. Maybe I'll finally get to see people! I'd like to see a baby whale, and I've never been to the surface before. It's exciting."

Shelly swallowed her octopus legs and licked her fingers. "I can't wait. I've always wanted to swim with whales."

"Swim with them? I could never do that!" Echo squealed. "My dad made me do a report on them last year in second grade. Do you know how big they are?"

Kiki nodded. "Whales are the largest creatures that have ever lived. That's why Mrs. Karp wants us to study them." Kiki didn't tell the girls that she was scared, but she was glad to hear that Echo was a little bit afraid too.

"They do this thing called bubble netting, where they trap their food!" Echo told her friends. Kiki stopped eating and stared at her.

Shelly shook her head. "Don't worry. Whales only eat fish and krill."

Echo flipped her pink mermaid tail. "Excuse me, but don't we look like big fish?"

Kiki looked down at her purple tail and gulped. Humpback whales were huge. All they had to do to swallow a mermaid was open their gigantic mouths wide. She was the smallest merkid in their class. What if a whale mistook her for a snack? Kiki closed her eyes for a moment and shuddered.

"I thought you wanted to see humans," Shelly said to Echo.

Echo smiled and pushed her dark, curly hair off her forehead. "You know it."

"Well, this could be your only chance," Shelly said. "My grandfather says humans love to watch whales."

Echo giggled. "Really? Then I can't miss the trip. I'd do almost anything to see a real, live human." She clasped her hands together, and Kiki could tell that Echo had forgotten her fear of whales in her excitement about seeing a human. Kiki felt totally alone with her secret. What was she going to do tomorrow? She just wasn't ready to share her fears.

"Now that that's settled, let's make Mr. Fangtooth smile today," Shelly told her friends. Ever since school had started a few weeks ago, the girls had tried to make the grumpy lunchroom worker cheer up. On the first day of school, they'd made funny faces at him. That had made him laugh, but it had also gotten them sent to the headmaster's office. Another time, Kiki and Shelly had walked on their hands in front of Mr. Fangtooth, but that had made him frown even more.

"I know," Kiki suggested, glad to think of something besides whales. "We could make weird sounds."

"What do you mean?" Shelly asked.

"At home, when it was time to sleep, my seventeen brothers would make silly noises one by one, and by the time they got to number seventeen, we were laughing so hard my dad would have to yell at everyone to go to sleep. But then he'd make the silliest sound of all, and we'd start laughing all over again." Remembering those good times made Kiki miss her family. The Trident Academy dorm room was a long way from her home.

Shelly giggled. "Let's try it." Shelly, Echo, and Kiki glided over to return their lunch trays. Mr. Fangtooth stood behind the rock counter, wearing his usual frown.

"*BBBBBLLLLLLLLSSSS,*" Kiki said as

she put down her tray. Her lips jiggled like a motorboat. Mr. Fangtooth didn't laugh, but everyone else in the lunchroom did.

"What was that?" shouted Rocky from a nearby table. "Did you hear what Kiki did?"

A table full of mergirls, headed by Pearl, pointed at Kiki and laughed. Kiki rushed back to her seat and covered her face with her long hair. "I'm so embarrassed," she said.

"Don't worry," Shelly told Kiki. "Rocky will find someone else to tease before long." Rocky was always making mischief.

"He'll be so excited about seeing the whales tomorrow, he won't think about you," Echo pointed out.

Kiki faked a smile for her friends. Trying to cheer up Mr. Fangtooth had made her forget about her fear of whales for a minute. Now she remembered again, and her stomach did a flip-flop.

She knew she was being silly. After all, whales were known for being gentle. But they were so *big*! And she was so small. She couldn't help how she felt any more than she could help how little she was.

Kiki put her head down. Her stomach was hurting, and it wasn't from the sushi. She had to think of a way to get out of the ocean trip tomorrow, and she had to think fast.

4

Killer Whale

AFTER SCHOOL, KIKI AND SHELLY met under Trident Academy's massive entrance dome. A glowing jellyfish chandelier lit up the colorful carvings on the ceiling. "Do you want to come to my dorm room while Echo's at Tail Flippers practice?" Kiki asked Shelly. Echo and Shelly had been friends since they'd been small fry, but Kiki had met the girls only a few weeks before, when school had started.

Shelly smiled. "Sure! I'd love to see your room." Shelly and Echo lived just a short swim away from Trident Academy, but many mergirls and merboys lived far from school and had to stay in the dormitory. Since Kiki's home was thousands of miles away near Asia, she lived in the dorm.

"It's not that exciting," Kiki admitted as they swam toward the girls' dorm. It was a short distance from the classrooms, down a long hallway, past a seaweed curtain marked MERGIRLS ONLY. The boys' rooms were on the opposite side of the school.

"I bet it's better than my apartment," Shelly said.

"At the People Museum?" Kiki asked.

"Yes," Shelly said. "I live with my grandfather. Our place is on the second floor." Shelly had lived with her grandfather since her parents died. The People Museum was filled with human objects of all sorts that had been found throughout the ocean. Merpeople came from all over the merkingdom to visit and study.

"Wow, that sounds neat," Kiki said as the mergirls floated down the hallway to the rooms. Some girls had decorated their seaweed doors with shell carvings of their families. One girl had even braided a pretty gold chain into her seaweed.

Shelly shook her head. "I think human stuff is boring. Echo loves it. But humans can't even swim."

"I've heard that some can," Kiki said.

"I hope so," Shelly said. "I can't imagine not being able to swim. Wouldn't it be horrible?"

Kiki stopped in front of a bright-blue shell curtain, pulled it back, and said, "Here's my room." One side of the room was filled with fluffy pink coral and tube sponges. Sparkling jewel anemones covered one wall. Merclothes littered the floor. "That's my roommate Wanda Slug's side," Kiki sighed as she looked at the mess.

"Is this yours?" Shelly asked, and pointed across the room to an enormous skeleton. "Is that a shark?"

"It's my bed!" Kiki explained. "It might look like a shark, but it's actually a killer whale. Come on, you can sit on it." The two girls crawled inside the ribs of the huge skeleton and sank into a nest of feathers.

"Wow, this is soft," Shelly said.

"My mermom saved gray heron feathers for five years to make this bed for me," Kiki said.

"You should come over to my apartment for dinner sometime," Shelly suggested. "My grandfather, Siren, would enjoy

meeting you. He loves learning about far-away waters."

"Your grandfather is the famous C. Siren, right?"

Shelly nodded. "Yes, it's kind of embarrassing."

"I think it would be cool to have a human expert in the family," Kiki said.

"I'm more interested in how you got this skeleton," Shelly said. "I bet Echo would never crawl inside this in a hundred years. Sharks and killer whales give her the creeps."

"Wanda hates it too. She says it gives her nightmares," Kiki told Shelly.

Shelly laughed. "I bet it was funny to see her face when she got a look at this." She gently patted one of the big rib bones.

"Are you scared of killer whales and sharks?" Kiki asked.

Shelly shrugged. "I'd be crazy not to be. They're pretty dangerous. But skeletons can't hurt you."

"That's true," Kiki said. "But what about whales? Are you scared of whales? They're enormous!" Kiki held her breath as she waited for Shelly's answer. Maybe she'd be able to tell Shelly how she really felt.

"Of course not. Why would I be?" Shelly said. "Whales are amazing. My grandfather taught me to speak the humpback dialect. I'm going to try to talk to one tomorrow."

"Really?" Kiki said. "I can speak humpback too!" Languages had always come easily to Kiki. Her father was an expert linguist who had taught her more than fifty undersea languages.

"Awesome. Tomorrow, let's talk to the humpbacks together," Shelly said as she got off the bed and floated to the front curtain. "Unless . . . unless you're afraid of whales. Are you?"

Kiki stared at Shelly. If Kiki told her the truth, Shelly might make fun of her and tell all the other third graders. How would Kiki ever go to class again?

"No way," Kiki answered. "I can't wait until tomorrow. I'll be there early!"

AFTER SHELLY LEFT, KIKI STAYED ON HER skeleton bed, safe and secure in the soft feathers. She had never felt smaller or more afraid. *What will I do about the class trip?* she thought. *Those whales are so gigantic! They could swallow someone my size in one gulp. I wish my parents were here to help me.*

Kiki put her hand under her pillow. She felt around for a few seconds, then took out a small coral-colored shell purse.

She opened it up. Inside was an orange starfish, tiny and delicate. Kiki held it up to her cheek. Her mother had given it to her before Kiki set off for Trident Academy, as a reminder of home and as a good-luck charm.

Kiki hoped its luck would help her tomorrow. She would need it more than ever.

Lucky Charm

THE NEXT MORNING, MRS. KARP'S
third-grade class arrived at
Trident Academy earlier than
usual. Everyone was excited about seeing
the whales, and there was a nervous buzz
in the swirling waters.

"Quiet down, quiet down, and listen

closely," Mrs. Karp told her students as they gathered outside the school. "I am handing each of you an ID tag to clip to your tail. This is your identification for the Shark Patrol." She handed out gold coins that had been folded to snap onto the students' tail fins. The coins were marked with the Trident Academy symbol.

Mrs. Karp was counting the mergirls and merboys. When she got to Shelly and Echo, she stopped. "Has either of you seen Kiki?"

Shelly answered, "No, Mrs. Karp. She told me yesterday she'd be here first thing in the morning."

"We won't leave without her, will we?"

Echo asked. "Please, let's just wait a few more minutes."

"No way! No way!" yelled Pearl. She dashed over to Mrs. Karp and the girls, her long pearl necklace trailing behind her. "Why should we let Kiki ruin the trip for us?"

Rocky joined in. "Yeah, Mrs. Karp. That little squirt is probably too scared to show up!"

Mrs. Karp clapped her hands three times. "We will wait two more minutes for Kiki, and then I'm afraid we'll have to go," she announced.

The class lined up two by two, Shelly and Echo in the rear. Just when the friends thought they would have to leave, they heard a splash behind them.

It was Kiki! Out of breath and looking as pale as mother-of-pearl, the little mergirl swam over to her friends, her head down.

"Where have you been?" Shelly said. "You had us worried."

Echo called out to Mrs. Karp, "Kiki's here! Let's go!"

Rocky looked over his shoulder and blurted out, "It's about time, shrimp! Who do you think you are, anyway—Neptune?"

"Rocky, that will be enough out of you," Mrs. Karp said sharply, and handed Kiki an ID tag. "I expect everyone to be on their best behavior."

"Are you feeling okay?" Shelly whispered to Kiki.

Kiki didn't lie. "No, I feel terrible. My stomach really hurts. That's why I'm so late."

"Maybe you shouldn't go," Shelly suggested. "I could stay with you."

Kiki smiled at her friend. She knew how badly Shelly wanted to see the whales.

"No," Echo said. "You go, Shelly. I'll take Kiki back to her dorm room."

Now Kiki smiled at Echo. Kiki knew that Echo hoped to see humans at the surface, even if just for a minute. Kiki couldn't ask her friends to give up this adventure. "That's okay. I'm sure I'll be fine." Kiki nodded at her teacher but held her arms around her stomach.

Mrs. Karp said to the class, "Now that Kiki's arrived, we can be on our way."

"All right!" Rocky shouted.

Mrs. Karp frowned and continued, "Listen carefully to these important instructions before we go. The sunlight is very strong, so keep your eyes closed at first. You may swim around to study the whales, but do not wander far. I will blow the conch horn when it's time to return below to school." Mrs. Karp patted the shell she had slung around her shoulder.

"I hope I can do this," Echo whispered. "I'm excited, but I'm also a little nervous."

Shelly patted Echo's arm. "Don't worry. We'll stay with you, right, Kiki?"

Kiki nodded. She thought Echo was brave to admit she was a tiny bit scared. Why couldn't she do the same?

"If there are humans around, I will blow two quick blasts on the shell and we will immediately submerge," Mrs. Karp added. No one needed to be told about the dangers of humans seeing merkids.

Echo's tail fluttered. "Let's hope there are humans and we can get a quick peek," she whispered to her friends.

Shelly nodded. "Grandpa told me humans like to watch humpbacks because they breach so often."

Shelly held out one hand to Echo, the other to Kiki. Kiki held on to Shelly, her shell purse swinging back and forth on her wrist. Kiki closed her eyes and wished to herself, *Please let me be brave.*

6

To the Top

REMEMBER, YOU MAY EXPERIENCE some discomfort on the way to the surface," Mrs. Karp told the class.

"Discomfort?" Kiki said, popping her eyes open and growing paler. "That doesn't sound good."

"It's all right," Shelly told her. "If your stomach feels worse, just tell us."

"Pay close attention to the whales," Mrs. Karp continued. "When we get back to school, you will write an essay on your experiences."

Rocky couldn't believe his ears. "An essay?" he groaned. "I knew this was too good to be true."

Kiki's throat got tighter and tighter. She felt as if she was going to pass out. She had seen whales from far away, and that had scared her. Now she was going to be close. Too close.

"When I count to three, you may swim to the surface," Mrs. Karp instructed. "One, two . . ."

"I think I'm going to throw up," Kiki whimpered to herself.

"Three!" Mrs. Karp said.

Several mergirls squealed. Some of the merboys cheered. But they all began rising in the water.

Merfolk live in the deep parts of the ocean, for protection from sharks and humans, and their eyes are used to the darkness. Even so, Kiki accidentally bumped an old merwoman, who shook her finger at the entire class. "You should be in school instead of knocking decent merfolk about."

"S-sorry," Kiki stammered.

"I've seen that lady near the Manta Ray Station," Shelly whispered.

Pearl and Wanda swam by. "What a grouch," Pearl said.

Wanda chimed in, "She should meet Mr. Fangtooth." Both mergirls laughed as they passed Kiki and her friends.

As the class got closer to the top, the water became clearer and quite bright.

"I'm feeling so strange," Echo spluttered.

"It's just your merbody adjusting to the different pressure in the water," Kiki said, remembering Dr. Mousteau's talk. She tried not to think about the whales up above. *I could still turn around and swim back to school,* she thought, but at that moment Shelly gripped Kiki's hand even more tightly.

"Close your eyes when you get to the top, so the sun won't blind you," Shelly said, reminding her friends of Mrs. Karp's surface instructions. "Open them carefully when you feel the sun's heat." The girls quickly closed their eyes.

Suddenly a loud shriek filled the water: *MOOOOOOOWHAWK!* The sound vibrated throughout Kiki's body.

"What's that noise?" Echo squeaked.

Kiki and Echo froze, but Shelly pulled them along. "It's the male humpback's song," she explained.

"Whales sing?" Echo asked, still squeezing her eyes shut. "I don't remember that from my second-grade report."

"Of course they sing," Shelly said excitedly. "Didn't you hear Dr. Mousteau's lecture? Grandpa told me they have the longest songs of any creature."

"I wonder if the humans are near and can hear it too," Echo said. "Swim faster so we can see for ourselves!"

Splash! The class broke through the surface of the ocean.

Kiki felt the burst of air on her face. She felt the pleasant warmth of the sun.

"Students, slowly open your eyes," Mrs. Karp instructed. Kiki did as she was told. Little by little, she opened her eyes.

And then she screamed and screamed!

No More Secrets

AAAAAH!" KIKI HOWLED OUT. "AAAAAH!"

"What's wrong?" Echo asked.

"What is that?" Kiki cried, and pointed to an oval object, shiny and huge.

"It's just an eye," Shelly laughed.

Kiki stopped screaming. "That's the biggest eyeball I've ever seen. Let's get out of here!" she said, and started to dive.

"Wait!" Shelly said. "Where are you going? What's wrong? I thought you liked whales."

Kiki started to cry. "Are you kidding? I'm petrified of them! I can't believe how big they are!"

Shelly and Echo looked at each other in surprise. "Why didn't you tell us?" Echo asked.

"Are you merladies all right?" Mrs. Karp asked, looking sharply at Kiki.

"Of course," Shelly quickly answered. "Kiki was just startled by how big this whale is."

Big didn't begin to describe the creature in front of Kiki. It was massive! Part of it floated above the water, and that part was as big as ten ordinary merhouses put together. The whale had large creases in its neck, and Kiki saw two huge scars on its side. For a moment, she felt sorry that the whale had been hurt. But then she went back to being scared again.

All around her, she could hear excited merkids shouting. "Wow, this one is like an island!" Rocky yelled.

"Ick!" Pearl screeched. "This one is covered with barnacles."

"Mine is the biggest one ever!" Adam shouted.

Kiki's eyes darted around. There must

have been at least twenty enormous humpbacks in this pod. Just then, one of them spouted water from its blowhole and showered the kids.

"I think that whale just spit on us!" Rocky yelled.

Kiki wanted to race home as fast as possible. But she was frozen in place. "Please don't tell anyone in class how scared I am," she whispered to Shelly and Echo. "Especially Pearl and Rocky. Pearl will make fun of me, and Rocky will tease me about how scared and small I am."

"Kiki," Shelly said, "don't worry. Relax. The whales won't hurt you. I promise."

"And we won't tell anyone your secret.

It's safe with us. I bet you a lot of merkids are frightened—more than you think," Echo said reassuringly. "I still am, a little bit."

Then Kiki heard Shelly speaking to the whale. And even though Kiki was terrified to the tip of her tail, she understood every word.

"Hello," Shelly said. "We are excited to meet you. May we touch you?"

"It winked at us!" Echo said with a nervous giggle.

"It's soooooo huge," Kiki said quietly. It was true. The girls weren't even as big as this whale's flippers. "One smack of its tail and we'd go flying."

"Don't worry. He's very gentle," Shelly said. She reached out her hand toward the enormous whale.

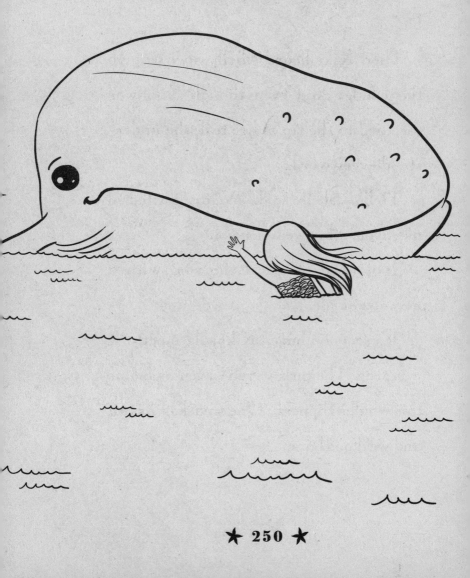

"Don't touch him!" Kiki yelled. But Shelly patted the whale and spoke to him again. The whale let out a sound like a moan.

"Really?" Shelly answered.

"What did he say?" Echo said. "Did Dr. Mousteau teach us those words?"

"He said, 'It's okay,'" Kiki explained.

"What's okay?" Echo asked.

"This," Shelly said. "Watch!"

Whale Ride

"SHELLY!" KIKI SCREAMED. "GET down off that whale! You'll get hurt!"

Shelly waved from the whale's back, her long red hair swirling around her. "He said we could all ride him."

"Wow! Come on, Kiki, let's do it. Maybe we'll see a boat or something human!" Echo said.

"We'll fall off!" Kiki answered.

"No, we won't," Shelly said. "Kiki, Echo, meet Mortimer. He said we can hold on to his bumps." Shelly pointed to three knobs on the back of the humpback's head.

"Well, you can just tell Mortimer that you are not going to do any such thing," Kiki said desperately. "Mrs. Karp will not allow it."

Kiki, Shelly, and Echo quickly looked at Mrs. Karp, who was trying to keep Rocky from pulling another whale's tail.

"She didn't say we couldn't ride a whale," Shelly said.

Echo grinned as Mortimer let out another long moan.

Kiki folded her arms over her chest. "Mrs. Karp never told us not to ride a shark, either, but we're smart enough not to try that."

"This is different," Shelly said. "Mortimer invited us."

"I'm doing it," Echo said, surprising both Shelly and Kiki. "I may never get another chance to do anything like this again."

"No!" Kiki squealed. "Echo, you're going to get up on that monster?"

"He's not a monster," Echo said. "Just because he's big doesn't mean he's a monster."

Kiki knew Echo was right. She didn't like feeling this way. Maybe it was because she was so small herself. Or maybe it was the scary stories her brothers had told her about whales. For whatever reason, she couldn't help being afraid.

"Come on," Shelly begged. "He's really nice. He wants you to come too."

"Well, maybe," Kiki muttered. Maybe if she held on to her lucky starfish, she could safely join Shelly and Echo. She went to open her purse to get her charm . . . but the purse wasn't there! Her purse and her lucky starfish were gone!

Kiki jumped away from the whale. *Oh no!* "I . . . I can't!" She really couldn't go, not without her good-luck charm.

"Then stand back," Shelly said, "because here we go!"

Echo jumped onto Mortimer, behind Shelly. "I can't believe I'm doing this," Echo said with a nervous giggle.

With a flip of his tail, Mortimer sprayed Kiki with a big splash of water. Then Mortimer, Echo, and Shelly were gone.

9

Deep-Sea Danger

WHEEE!" SHELLY, ECHO, AND Mortimer dove deep into the ocean.

"Come back!" Kiki yelled, but her voice was lost in whale song. All around her, whales sang. Kiki held her hands over her ears to block out the noise. "We've got to stop them. They're going to be hurt! Won't someone help me?" Kiki cried.

Everyone was too busy talking, touching, splashing, and learning about the other whales. No one heard Kiki. She couldn't see Mrs. Karp anywhere.

"I have to find her," Kiki said. She rushed between the huge whales, searching desperately for her teacher. "Where did she go?"

With no sign of Mrs. Karp, Kiki was frantic. She realized she would have to be the one to save her friends—there wasn't a second to waste. Up went her tail, and down went her head into the water.

Whoosh!

Mortimer raced by. Kiki swam as fast

as she could, but a small mergirl is no match for a speeding humpback whale.

As she got closer, she heard her friends screaming.

"Oh no!" Kiki said. "They're in danger! I knew it!

"Help!" she yelled. "Somebody help me!" *If only I hadn't lost my starfish,* she thought, *none of this would have happened!*

"I can help," a voice said.

Kiki came face to face with . . . a whale!

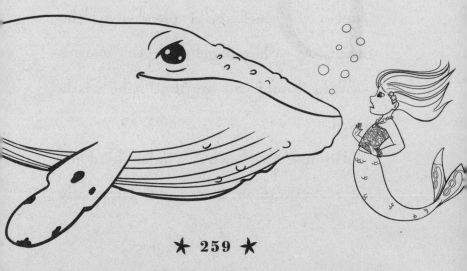

A Big Decision

"**D**ON'T EAT ME! DON'T HURT me!" Kiki pleaded in the humpback dialect.

"Why would you say that?" the whale asked.

"Because that's what whales do. They eat everything in their sight. Especially small things. Like me," Kiki whimpered, and backed away. This whale was only half as big as Mortimer, but that was still too large for Kiki.

"Please don't leave," the little whale said. "I've never met a mergirl before. And all these merkids are splashing and making so much noise, they're scaring me!"

Kiki stopped. "What? You're scared? How could something as tremendous as you be scared of something as little as me?"

"I'm just a baby whale," he said. "But my uncle Mortimer always told me to help all creatures of the sea. And you were calling for help. What's wrong?"

Kiki couldn't believe her ears. "*Wow!*" she said. "You sure are big for a baby."

Surprising herself, she didn't swim away. After all, the baby whale was kind of cute. Kiki continued, "Your uncle sped away with my friends on his back. They're in danger, and I've got to find them now!"

"If you want, you can hold on to my tail and we'll go look for them," said the young whale. "But you should know that my uncle would never harm anyone. You can ask any of the whales in our pod."

Kiki wasn't sure what to do. She didn't want to touch or go near this whale, but she had to save Shelly and Echo. Slowly she put her fingers around his left fluke. He didn't feel icky at all. Kiki was surprised to find that his fin was pretty smooth.

"My name is Orman. Hold tightly—I won't swim too fast," he assured her.

"I-I'm K-Kiki," she stammered as Orman dove deep into the water. At first, Kiki was so nervous she squeezed her eyes shut. She felt the water rushing past her cheeks. After a few minutes, she dared to open one eye.

The undersea world swirled by in a colorful blur. It wasn't scary at all. It was really very pretty. Kiki was having so much fun, she almost forgot she was searching for her friends. Suddenly a mass of bubbles swirled around her and Orman.

"Kiki!" Shelly and Echo yelled.

"Shelly! Echo!" Kiki shouted back. "Where have you been?" She shook a finger at them. "You could have been injured! You could have lost a fin! You are both so lucky Orman and I were able to find you."

Mortimer let out a hearty laughing sound. Shelly and Echo joined in.

"What are you all laughing at?" Kiki asked. "This is serious!"

"Save us from what?" Echo asked.

"From . . . from that huge whale," Kiki said. "He—he might eat you."

Shelly smiled. "Oh, Kiki, thank you for being so brave and trying to help us. But we don't need saving."

"You don't?" Kiki said.

"No," Shelly said. "We were having fun."

"Then why were you screaming when Mortimer took off with you?" Kiki asked.

"Screaming? We were squealing because we were so excited," Echo told her. "But I'm sorry we left you alone. I forgot that you weren't feeling well."

"And that you were scared," Shelly said. "But, Kiki, if you're so terrified of humpbacks, why are you with one now?"

Kiki looked from Orman to her friends and explained, "His name is Orman, and he's only a young whale. I would never ride on his back. I only held on to his fluke, and he wasn't swimming all that fast. . . ."

Shelly laughed. Then Echo. And then Mortimer and Orman. Kiki was mad for a second, but then she laughed too.

"Well, at least we don't have to ride the whales anymore," she said. "I'm not as frightened as I was at first, and Orman is really nice, but now we can all go home."

Shelly and Echo smiled and shook their heads.

"There's one more adventure today," Echo said. "Mortimer is going to breach with us on his back."

"No!" Kiki said.

"Yes!" Shelly said. "And you can do it too."

"I would never," Kiki said.

"If you don't do it, you'll never know the fun you're missing," Echo said. "This may be your only chance to do something this exciting."

Shelly held out her hand. "Come on, Kiki."

Kiki looked at Shelly's hand and made

her decision. "I can't. I'm terrified of such a large creature," she said in the humpback dialect. "I'm sorry, Mortimer; I'm sorry, Orman, but I just can't help myself. Maybe it's because I've always been so little for my age." Kiki began to cry. "And . . . I lost my lucky starfish charm."

"We'll help you look for it," Shelly said immediately.

"No," Kiki said, wiping her tears. "You go have fun. You may never get this chance again."

"I'll help you," Orman told Kiki.

Kiki couldn't help smiling at the cute whale. Once again, she held on to his tail. He swam toward the bottom of the ocean. Every couple of yards, he would stop so

Kiki could look behind the red-and-yellow coral reefs, on the spiny purple sea urchins, and around the sea cucumbers.

"Orman, do you think we'll ever find it?" Kiki asked him. "It's special because my mermom gave it to me."

And just then, on top of a barrel sponge, Kiki spotted her shell purse!

"Stop, Orman! I see it!" Kiki said. She swam to the barrel sponge, picked up her purse, and took out the starfish.

"This is my lucky charm, Orman," she said, showing him the five-pointed star. She knew she would never have found it without his help. "And you're my lucky friend. Now let's go for that ride!"

11

Flying

CAREFULLY, KIKI GOT ON
Orman's back and grabbed
a knob on his head.

"Don't worry, Kiki," Orman said. "I
won't go too fast."

Up they swam, back to Shelly, Echo,

and Mortimer. Kiki's friends couldn't believe their eyes!

"Kiki, you look awesome!" Shelly cheered. "Are you ready? Hold on tight."

"Ready!" Kiki answered. "Thanks for waiting for me." She was still a little nervous, but she knew Orman and her friends would look out for her.

Mortimer spoke to Orman, and Orman slapped his tail. Suddenly water zoomed past the girls' faces and they were propelled toward the surface much faster than any merperson could ever swim.

"Aaaaah!" screamed Kiki, her eyes shut tight.

"Mrs. Karp!" Rocky yelled. "Look at Kiki, Shelly, and Echo!"

A huge gasp came from the rest of their class. "Girls!" Mrs. Karp called.

Kiki heard Rocky and Mrs. Karp, but she couldn't let go. She held on as Orman cleared the water and they soared into the air.

"Wow!" Shelly said from Mortimer's back. "This is amazing. Kiki, open your eyes. You don't want to miss this."

Kiki opened one eye as the wind blew her long dark hair. Mortimer and Orman had breached together. "It's beautiful," Kiki breathed.

As far as she could see, blue water stretched all around. Up above, bright

sky matched the sparkling sea.

"We're swimming in the air!" Echo screamed. And they were. For just a minute. And then they started falling.

"Don't let go!" Shelly yelled.

Kiki squeezed Orman's knob hard. The water felt like a rock when they hit it, and it was all Kiki could do to stay on Orman's back. But she did. And right beside her, she could see that Shelly and Echo had stayed on Mortimer.

When they were safely back under the water, Echo giggled. "We did it!"

Kiki couldn't believe it. Thanks to Orman and her merfriends, she had done something she'd never thought she could do. She hugged Orman. "Thank you, my lucky pal. I hope I get to see you again."

Orman winked at Kiki, and Kiki knew she had a friend for life.

Trouble Time?

"YOU ARE IN SO MUCH TROUBLE!" Rocky told the girls after their whale rides.

"Yeah," added Pearl. "No more ocean trips for you. Ha!"

Mrs. Karp blew the conch shell, signaling that it was time to leave. All the merstudents gathered around her. Kiki gulped when Mrs. Karp glared at her.

"All right, class," Mrs. Karp said. "Let's descend."

Nobody said a word as they swam downward together. It took a minute for their eyes to adjust to the darkness, and Echo jumped when a small basketweave cusk-eel slithered by her.

"Let's assemble in the classroom," Mrs. Karp told the class. "We have a few more minutes left before the end of the school day."

The merstudents groaned. "I thought she would let us go home early," Shelly whispered.

"Nope," Rocky said, swimming by the three mergirls. "She wants to yell at you first."

Kiki glanced at Mrs. Karp, who had a serious look on her face. Kiki was afraid Rocky was right.

"What do you think Mrs. Karp will do

to us?" Echo whispered as the class floated
down the hallway.

Kiki shrugged. Her parents wouldn't
mind that she'd ridden Orman, but they

would be upset if she got in trouble at school. They always told her to do her best in her studies, but that even if she couldn't get good grades, she could behave herself. It had been a huge honor for her to win a Trident Academy scholarship. She was the first one in her family to attend the prestigious school. It would be terrible if she was sent home in disgrace. Kiki held her breath as Mrs. Karp addressed the class.

"You may take a few minutes to write about the humpback whales," she said. All the merkids bent over their pieces of seaweed to begin their essays. Everyone except Rocky.

"What about Kiki, Shelly, and Echo?"

Rocky asked. "Aren't they going to get sent to the headmaster for riding those whales?"

Mrs. Karp stared at Rocky and then at the girls. Kiki felt sick to her stomach again. "There is one regrettable part about today's ocean trip," Mrs. Karp said.

Kiki waited anxiously as Mrs. Karp paused.

"I am terribly disappointed that I did not get to ride the whales," Mrs. Karp told them. "I have always wanted to breach with a humpback."

Kiki looked at her teacher in surprise. "You mean we aren't in trouble?" she asked.

Mrs. Karp shook her head. "Not this

time." Then she smiled and continued, "But if the humpbacks ever come back, I expect a ride."

"Of course," Kiki quickly told her teacher. "Orman, my new whale friend,

would be delighted." Kiki's lucky starfish charm sat on top of her desk. With the charm, and with the help of Shelly, Echo, and Orman, she had faced her biggest fear. Kiki smiled and wrote her essay. She couldn't wait for her next big adventure at Trident Academy.

Class Reports

★ ✦ ★

MY ESSAY ON HUMPBACK WHALES

By Shelly Siren

Today I did something I have only dreamed about. I got to breach on top of a humpback whale. It was amazing. The whale, whose name is Mortimer, was so big he made me feel like a tiny speck of the littlest krill.

MY ESSAY ON HUMPBACK WHALES

By Echo Reef

I learned that humpback whales sing very loud songs. I think their songs are kind of sad, like they are missing a loved one. Humpback whales have the longest songs of any sea creature. They are also very friendly to mermaids. I was sorry we didn't get to see a human, but I will never forget riding a whale.

MY ESSAY ON HUMPBACK WHALES

By Rocky Ridge

At first, I thought the humpback whales were really ugly. After all, they have bumps all over their faces. But when I saw one jump out of the water, I thought it was really pretty.

MY ESSAY ON HUMPBACK WHALES
By Pearl Swamp

Humpback whales are the biggest, grossest, most disgusting creatures in the ocean. They are noisy and stinky. I hope I never have to see another one ever again. I don't think it's fair that some people in our class didn't get in trouble for doing something they shouldn't have done. And it wasn't right that they didn't share with us. If one person got to ride on a whale, then everyone should get to ride on a whale. It's only fair.

MY ESSAY ON HUMPBACK WHALES
By Kiki Coral

I was terrified of being around the biggest creatures in the ocean. I thought because they were big, they would be mean. But they were very nice and understanding.

I enjoyed looking around when we breached. I could see the blue of the ocean going on forever. All around us, the sky matched the blue. I felt like a seabird soaring high above the world.

Mrs. Karp, I hope Mortimer and his nephew, Orman, come back for a visit. It would be fun to ride on a whale with you! I would still be a little scared, but not terrified.

The Mermaid Tales Song

REFRAIN:

Let the water roar

Deep down we're swimming along

Twirling, swirling, singing the mermaid song.

VERSE 1:

Shelly flips her tail

Racing, diving, chasing a whale

Twirling, swirling, singing the mermaid song.

VERSE 2:

Pearl likes to shine

Oh my Neptune, she looks so fine

Twirling, swirling, singing the mermaid song.

VERSE 3:

Shining Echo flips her tail

Backward and forward without fail

Twirling, swirling, singing the mermaid song.

VERSE 4:

Amazing Kiki

Far from home and floating so free

Twirling, swirling, singing the mermaid song.

Author's Note

OCEANS ARE FANTASTIC PLACES filled with incredible creatures, like humpback whales. Check out the fangtooth or the hairy angler if you want to see something really creepy! Maybe there are other living things we haven't found yet that are even more amazing—like mermaids! Read on for some facts about the ocean animals mentioned in this book. Hope I didn't miss any! Tell me about your favorite sea creature by writing me on the Kids Talk to Debbie section of www.debbiedadey.com. Is your favorite a baby whale, like Orman?

My nephew Damon Gibson actually swam with humpbacks and told me it was one of the coolest experiences of his life. If you don't know how to swim, I hope you'll learn. After all, you may get to swim with whales one day!

Take care,
Debbie Dadey

Glossary

BARREL SPONGE: This huge sponge is large enough for a person to hide inside!

BASKETWEAVE CUSK-EEL: This eel has been found at depths of 26,000 feet, the greatest depth for any fish.

BOTTLENOSE DOLPHIN: These dolphins vary in color from pale blue to slate gray. They "talk" using whistles, clicks, and squeaks.

CONCH: The conch shell has been collected because of its beauty, and the conch itself has been eaten for food. Conchs are now at risk for extinction.

FANGTOOTH: This deep-water fish has a large head and massive teeth.

GRAY HERON: This gray-backed bird will wait patiently for a long time and then stab quickly with its bill to catch a fish.

GREAT WHITE SHARK: Great whites have been known to attack humans, but we are not their natural prey. Scientists believe that the attacking shark mistakes the human for a seal or a turtle. It is important to stay out of the ocean during early-morning and early-evening hours, when sharks are more likely to feed.

HAIRY ANGLER: Only a few of these weird-looking fish have ever been seen. The hairy angler has a huge mouth, little eyes, and long, thin fin rays, making it look like a bald man with a few wild hairs.

HUMPBACK WHALE: Humpback whales grow to be between forty and fifty feet long. How big is that? Many kids' bedrooms are around ten feet long. That would mean one whale could be five times as long as your bedroom!

JEWEL ANEMONE: These colorful creatures make a fabulously colorful display on underwater cliffs and can be any color, although pink and yellow are common.

KILLER WHALE: Killer whales are not whales at all. They are the largest member of the dolphin family. Despite their name, killer whales are not known for attacking people— or mermaids—in the wild.

KRILL: Antarctic krill are very important in the southern ocean food chain.

OCTOPUS: The small blue-ringed octopus makes enough toxic spit to kill a human! It has little bright blue circles all over its body.

PINK CORAL: Corals are some of the brightest reef creatures. They can be pink, red, orange, yellow, or white.

POLKA-DOT BATFISH: The batfish is an oddly shaped fish that uses its fins to walk over the ocean floor.

PURPLE SEA URCHIN: This small urchin loves to eat kelp. In fact, urchins have destroyed parts of giant kelp forests.

SEA CUCUMBER: This wormlike creature eats mud and sand!

SHRIMP: There are many types of shrimp in the ocean. The peacock mantis shrimp is brightly colored and lives in warm water near reefs.

STARFISH: The vivid colors of starfish scare off some predators.

TUBE SPONGE: This pinkish sponge looks like fingers reaching up from the sea floor.

FIND OUT WHAT HAPPENS IN THE NEXT . . .

Mermaid Tales

★Debbie Dadey★

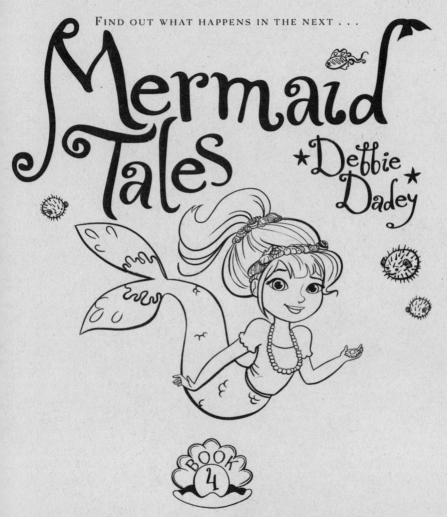

BOOK 4

Danger in the Deep Blue Sea

Late-Breaking News!

O H MY NEPTUNE!" PEARL
Swamp shrieked as she
swam into the huge front
hallway of Trident Academy. "Did you
see the newspaper this morning?"

Wanda Slug, Pearl's good friend, shook
her head. "No, I didn't," she said. "I had

to finish my homework before school."
The two mergirls floated out of the way
of some fourth-grade merboys who zoomed
past them.

Trident Academy was a prestigious
school in Trident City. Third-grade

through tenth-grade merkids came from all over the ocean to study in the enormous clamshell. The front hall alone was big enough for a humpback whale to take a nap in.

Pearl's blond hair and long strand of pearls swirled in the water as merstudents rushed around her to get to their classrooms. "My dad made me read the front page," she told Wanda. "You'll never believe it! There have been shark sightings in Trident City!"

"What?" Wanda gasped. "Are you kidding? That's terrible." Sharks were the number one danger to the merpeople community.

Pearl's green eyes widened. "I'm serious.

I couldn't even swim here by myself. My father hired a Shark Patrol Guard to escort me to and from school."

Wanda shuddered. "I'm glad I live in the Trident Academy dorm. I wouldn't want to be swimming home with a shark on my tail." Both girls looked at their own mertails and wiggled them gently. Neither girl noticed that the front hall was almost empty of merstudents.

Pearl slapped her gold tail on the shell floor and folded her arms across her chest. "This is ridiculous. What's wrong with this place? Can't they keep scary sharks from chasing people? Something should be done."

"Yeah, but what can we do?" Wanda said. "We're just third graders."

Pearl twisted her necklace in her fingers. "I hate being scared and I hate having a Shark Guard. My dad might not even let me go to Tail Flippers practice if things get worse!"

"No!" Wanda gasped. Tail Flippers was the school's dance and gymnastics team.

Pearl sighed. "I don't know what I'm going to do, but I'm going to do something. I refuse to let sharks ruin my life."

"Uh-oh," Wanda said, finally noticing the empty hall. "We'd better get to class or *Mrs. Karp* will ruin our lives!"

2

Shark Patrol

PEARL AND WANDA MADE IT to class just as the conch shell sounded. Pearl swam up to her teacher's desk. "Mrs. Karp, did you hear the terrible news?" she asked. "A shark has been spotted in Trident City! Can't something be done?"

Echo Reef, one of the third graders, raised her hand. "Is it true?" she said in a trembling voice.

"My grandfather saw it in the paper," Shelly Siren said. She nervously flicked her blue tail.

"Are we in danger here at Trident Academy?" Kiki Coral asked. She was the smallest mergirl in the third grade.

The twenty merstudents looked to their teacher for an answer. Mrs. Karp ran a hand through her green hair. "I am sure the Shark Patrol is doing everything in their power to protect us. We can't panic," she said.

"But what if it's not *enough*?" Pearl cried. The thought of sharks swimming near the school made her feel sick.

"Remember the first rule of shark safety and you should be fine," Mrs. Karp said, pointing to the Shark Safety Rules chart that hung from a seaweed curtain. "Shelly, please read rule number one."

Shelly cleared her throat and said in a shaky voice, "NEVER SWIM ALONE." Pearl sniffed. Why did Mrs. Karp always call on Shelly? Was it just because her grandfather was a famous human expert? Pearl knew she could read just as well as Shelly.

Rocky Ridge, one of the merboys in class, piped up, "Don't cry, Pearl. A shark wouldn't want to bite you. You're more sour than sweet."

"You're the only sour one around here," Pearl said, sticking her tongue out at him. "I bet you're just as scared as I am!"

"Class, please pass your homework in," Mrs. Karp instructed, trying to change the subject.

Their schoolwork was done on small pieces of seaweed and written with orange sea pens and octopus ink. All around the classroom the merkids handed seaweed to the merstudent in front of them. Everyone except Rocky, who tapped his thumbs on his rock desk and whistled a shark song. Several mergirls whispered nervously about the shark.

"Mrs. Karp? Should we be worried?" Kiki asked.

Mrs. Karp looked at the frightened faces of the mergirls and merboys. She didn't lie to her merstudents. "Of course, when you live in the ocean, as we do, you must always be on the lookout for dangerous creatures who want to eat you. It's part of the ocean life cycle."

"That's just disgusting," Pearl said. "I don't want to be part of a life cycle."

"You mean if we lived on land, we wouldn't have to worry about sharks?" Echo asked. The whole class knew how much Echo loved everything about humans. She hoped to get the chance to see one someday.

"Only if you went into the water," Mrs. Karp said. "That's the one advantage humans have over us."

"Maybe I want to be human, then," Pearl snapped.

The entire class gasped. Merpeople were not supposed to speak like that. There was an ancient legend about a beautiful mermaid who had turned into a human. No one knew what had happened to her, but there were creepy stories about a witch chasing her. Merkids told scary tales about it late at night during sleepover parties.

"Humans can't even breathe underwater!" Rocky said, breaking the tension.

"That's right," Kiki agreed. "I heard they even drink water!"

Everyone in the class laughed at the silliness of that idea. Drinking water! Why would anyone do that?